The Procurements of Sonny Valentine:
All Kinds of Stories

Short stories from
Detective Theo & Doctor Valentico

Other Books From Future Publishing House:

Asleep in the Skies by Sonny Valentine
The Lost Poet of Woodlawn
Men, Women & Robots
Boy Meets Bot (A One-Act Play)
REDACTED

Copyright © 2020 Future Publishing House and Shaun Vain

All rights reserved. No portion of this book may be reproduced in any form without permission from the publisher, except as permitted by U.S. copyright law.
For all permissions, contact FUTURE PUBLISHING HOUSE.
Go to www.futurepublishinghouse.com to connect.

ISBN: 978-1-953818-01-0

Library of Congress Control Number: 2020921433

Publisher's Cataloging-in-Publication Data
Vain, Shaun 1988–
The Procurements of Sonny Valentine: all kinds of stories/ Detective Theo & Doctor Valentico Series, created by Shaun Vain.
    174 p.
    ISBN 978-1-953818-01-0
1. Fiction—Detective and mystery stories. 2. Fiction—Short stories. I. Vain, Shaun. II. Title. III. Series name.

PS3622.A.36 D.484 2020
810.54 ddc   LCCN: 2020921433

10 9 8 7 6   FPS   e 4 3 2 1
10 18 24 23 22 21 20
First edition.

This book is a work of fiction. All characters, including its author, are a creation of S. Vain. Any similarities to persons living, dead, or imaginary are coincidental.

Series logo designed by Mary Parrish.

THIS IS A FUTURE PUBLISHING HOUSE PUBLICATION
BALTIMORE, MARYLAND

Table of Contents

Prologue written by Sonny Valentine
... pg. viii

CASE ONE: The Missing Son of a Barber
... pg. 1

CASE TWO: Bread Crumb Trails
... pg. 26

CASE THREE: A Day at the Fair Sparks Intrigue
... pg. 45

CASE FOUR: The Case of Sylvan Trappers
... pg. 57

CASE FIVE: Getting Help from a Pimp and His "Real" Girl
... pg. 79

CASE SIX: Shaken Apart
PART I
... pg. 93

PART II
... pg. 111

CASE SEVEN: A Story of a Missing Child at the Border
... pg. 138

Prologue

FEW people are able to withstand my journalistic style that includes only the bare minimal mention of my actual being at the place where the story happens.

In *The Procurements of Sonny Valentine*, I include little of my actual physical appearance at the scene. I leave myself entirely out the story.

If you cast aside the feud you have with how it ought to be, perhaps you will get along with some of the characters in this presentation. Though, if you slam your fist and shout above the perching winged composition before you, so be it. You'll find you align with some of these characters too, mind you.

I feel that it's worth repeating that although you might appreciate me because I'm as tall as most doorways, I typically crowd the scene with my tape recorder and pen always moving to notate every action and what the people around me say.

Sometimes, I am even able to produce the entire story as an exact transcription from the source. Take Case One as an example, for it was told to me by Captain Larry Stegner. So much of the story is in Stegner's own words and not mine, which is why I give credit to the sources in the first place.

Mind you, he told me the story on one occasion, and the same goes for the rest of the moments that I missed, and the thoughts people have revealed to me throughout my years as a journalist.

I'm similar to a historian, or an archeologist. I'm a documentarian of humanity.

I make it easy and enjoyable to read.

Please bear in mind the following:

It's done with the hope that someone like you would find it and read it to know the actual people behind the tidal reformations weren't a bunch of political folks like the group (you'll hear Oriel discuss later) on board when the Elixiumbrium crystal first disappeared.

. . . They were real people.

They were doctors, detectives, and scientists, and they were public servants too, but ultimately they were people.

This is their story. All together their own.

Until my last words, Yours,

Sonny Valentine

CASE ONE:

A true-crime story, as told by L. Stegner, Captain, the Montréal Police Department.

They were driving around near Cynthia's office because he always put it on his route when he was with the Force. They were over near the Basilique Notre-Dame de Montréal when Detective Theodore Bryant thought it would be a good time to get some caffeine in his system. Their squad car with 413 on the roof pulled off. His partner at the time was McKindley actually. When they pulled off to go in an artisan shop on Place d'Armes, it was to meet with another pair of badges.

Gerald and his partner by the name of Howie Windhurst were present at Xavier's Artisan, a coffee and sandwich shop near the basilica. When the call came in for everyone to respond, all four sergeants were the first to show up at the pier. There was already a crowd gathered there, around the opening from the street, where the colored paint was sprayed from the road to the new sculpture on the Jasques-Cartier Pier. Those side-by-side, double-yellow lines were long enough that the responding police didn't get out of their cars to follow the trail on foot. Instead, they followed the paint trails in their squad cars, all the way down the boardwalk to the end of the pier. That's where the new artist to declare Montréal as "the Artist Mecca of America" recently dedicated an extravagant collage.

Right in the middle of the double-yellow lines going up (and around him) onto the painting (and behind him) to wrap around the sculpture, was the son of the town barber, Virgil Brewer, with paint on his jacket too.

"The kid's passed out with enough drugs and alcohol in his system to keep him calm," said Theodore to the group of sergeants. The teenager was forced onto a stretcher and had to be tied down before the emergency medical team could make adequate observations.

"Well," said Sergeant McKindley to Howie Windhurst, "looks like Virgil got carried away at the sculpture's grand opening."

Bugsy, the artist who's sculpture was destroyed, arrived at the scene moments after the ambulance rushed away with Virgil Brewer. He knelt down in front of the sculpture in an act of humility before his creation, and he wept.

"He's just on time—if you catch my drift," said Sergeant Theodore Bryant.

"I don't get it," said Howie Windhurst.

"Me either," said Gerald to McKindley.

"Don't look at me," said McKindley.

"He's your partner," said Gerald.

"I mean," said Theo, "Bugsy is just in time to see what new additions Virgil has done to his sculpture."

Howie Windhurst sighed and said, "Yeah, but Virgil ain't no artist."

"He's the drunken son of a washed up barber."

DETECTIVE THEO & DOCTOR VALENTICO
IN
THE MISSING SON OF A BARBER

AN AFTERNOON THAT FELT SWOLLEN WITH DELAY.

The sun pouring through the sky lights at the Central Montréal Police Station helped everyone stay in their chairs with arms folded. That was until a squirrel-spirited man rushed into the precinct and startled everyone with pressing news. It was loud enough to get Theodore out of the file room when he still had clerk duty, during an afternoon just out of his rookie year. That was one of the other roles he had to fill in order for the department to warrant his restructuring of Internal Investigations.

The fellow moved his grey cap in circles enough to get on McKindley's nerves and before the guy could say a word McKindley asked him to keep his hands "stiller than . . . a wet flame." That prompted the man to say: "Old man down the street needs some help if you boys sitting around."

Theodore Bryant stated to a few others, "Clearly he's sick."

"What makes you think that?" someone asked.

"I don't know what's making him act that way, but look at his palms clenching," said Bryant. Theodore could also tell something based off of the man's perfectly hairless neckline: "He just got out of the barber."

"Some of that trembling is natural," said the crime scene investigator and forensics analyst Victoria Carteret. "Look at the way his hands shake . . . even when they're at rest."

In fact the man brought with him a case of his own that put Detective Bryant looking for the barber that shaved that man's face, for according to the man with the grey cap, the barber's child ran away with money he stole from his own father. The man with the grey cap bowed his head and bobbed back up to say his own name was Alfansio Maynard, and he said, "My worries are for the child's safety, of course."

Sergeant Ross McKindley took down all the information he could handle. Maynard wrote in the logbook under "Purpose for Visit" that he was "a concerned neighbor, looking out for neighborhood business interests." He further explained, "I worry about the sanity of my neighbor to not report the crime himself."

Bryant approached the desk from behind McKindley and asked, "Why did it go unreported?"

"Family, of course," said Maynard, "but the teenage boy.... He is a criminal and not to be trusted."

Maynard agreed to accompany Bryant and McKindley back to his neighborhood. McKindley rode with Maynard, and he recorded some notes in a small pad kept in his pocket. Meanwhile, he let his radio take care of relaying most of the things Maynard said. "He had the shop closed when I got there, but he agreed to clean me up since we go back so many years," said Maynard.

"Would you say that you're friends of each other?" inquired McKindley.

"Yes," said Maynard. "Indeed. I helped him figure out how to get around some building violations, uh— and he agreed to look out his window to make sure my shop wasn't getting robbed from time to time. Now, look at his own son.... After all those years."

The cleanly shaven Alfansio Maynard described the day as he remembered while I finished searching with nearby departments to make sure there wasn't already a report on file.

Theodore Bryant followed Maynard's station wagon in a patrol car. They passed by Bryant's last apartment that probably made him think of moving in with Valentico, but then he focused on the case when McKindley pressed on his radio to let Bryant and everyone else hear what Maynard was saying:

"It's usually lovely that side of the street since it's where shops get more extravagant, and people come from the village all around... constantly.... Coming by our shops to get nicer things they can't get outside of this... great city. The fancy throw rugs. Handmade ties made of the finest fabrics. Suits tailored by strong hands. Even with the vandals spraying the bricks a different color. That vandal who put up that junk on the pier— I don't mind looking at that, of course.... That's art. But this yellow paint they got all over the place. At first, I said it made the street glow—I thought they did it to spruce up on account of all the shops being luxury shops and it being the holiday season."

"What holiday is that?" asked McKindley.
"For every holiday you have to look good, son," said Maynard. His words brought a cheerful smile to McKindley's glum face. "If you have a shop, you got to make it the best damn looking shop you can make it. Look out for the new floor mat in front of my beautiful doors that are custom designed by Taylor's Antique on Main."
"I will," said McKindley. "So there's graffiti, and what else?"
"This morning there was much broken glass," said Maynard. "Enough to cut yourself on." He scratched his chin with his thumbnail.
"The glass is on account of the robbery," McKindley spoke his thoughts aloud. "Do you suppose?"
"Right," said Maynard.
The police radio on McKindley's person came on loudly when I spoke to say: "No reports on robberies in that district . . . . None today." That prompted Maynard to say: "Of course there aren't any reports. The boy . . . is his son."
"Of course," sympathized McKindley, "they have— the owner, in this case Mr. Brewer, has the right not to report it. Just as you have the right to do what you're doing. Do you know . . . what all was missing?"
"The register was cleared out," said Maynard, "but there's never much in it anyway."
"Anything else?" asked McKindley.
"Monty said he didn't have his scissors when I asked for a haircut," said the shopkeeper as he pulled into a private parking spot on the street marked for residents only. "Maybe they were stolen too. A junkie can get a lot of money for some new professional grade shears." Out from Maynard came a disgusting amount of glee that was cause for me to send another car out to the same neighborhood. The room of police looked at me for commands when we heard the strange Alfansio Maynard's cackling, overheard thanks to McKindley's open radio transmission.

5

Inside the barbershop business was slow but a regular customer was there to see a barber for a haircut and shave. The barber cleaned his scissors while the customer picked out a magazine to read from the waiting area. Near the door of the shop a man sat behind a counter and fiddled with the cash register drawer. He held a hammer and chisel, which he tapped gently. The antique register's drawer changed shape with each tap. He tried to slide the drawer closed and it became stuck shut.

Jed said, "Monsieur Brewer, I got an idea for you."

"I'm listening," said Brewer.

"You ought to try putting a booth at the fair this year. A dunking booth, that is. Get a dunk win a free haircut. You'll get this place fixed up. You'll see."

"Good thinking," said Monty Brewer. "You going to dunk for us?"

Bryant parked in front of the barbershop with his flashing lights on but no siren. Meanwhile, McKindley swiftly unlatched his defensive mechanisms in case the old shopkeeper became any stranger.

"You know you could have imposed upon your friendly neighbor to come in to file the report, Mr. Maynard?" McKindley said, trying to arouse any impatience the old shopkeeper might have been carrying.

"Not if he didn't want to press charges," snapped Maynard. "It's hard to get anyone over here. Why is it so hard?"

"Well, sir," said McKindley. "I'll ask a few questions when I meet him." Maynard waited with his station wagon while McKindley checked in with Bryant, but first he said to Maynard, "I need to ask my partner something about another case we're working."

"Could you take the statement while I stick with Maynard?" McKindley asked Bryant. "The guy is acting pretty strange."

"We're sending a car over," I said over the radio when I sorted out who I'd send. "Take the statement and keep everyone cool. Alight, Bryant?"

"Sounds great," said Theodore Bryant. "Hey, maybe I'll help him sweep up the broken glass while I'm at it!"

"You might find out something else," I told him. "Listen to your instincts. My instincts say something is wrong with our friend here."

"I thought the same thing," said Bryant.

"I don't see anything amiss," sighed McKindley, "apart from not getting that haircut."

The old shopkeeper put his grey cap on and waved the two sergeants over to his shop. They crossed the street, Rue Notre-Dame Oest, together and walked over to the barbershop with Maynard.

While McKindley waited outside with Maynard, Sergeant Theodore Bryant arrived on the scene inside the barber's shop. The shop was open for business, like usual, though the window was not in place. The empty hole in the wall revealed the barber inside using an electric shaver that buzzed loudly enough to be heard by anyone on the street and sidewalk.

Sergeant Bryant patiently sat inside the shop. He swirled his long coattail around his thighs to keep it from touching the tile floor. The place was cleaner than most barbershops in town, but there were a few tufts of hair below the chair nearest to Bryant. Upon sitting, he noticed a unique array of magazines, very few of the type that could be found in an average drugstore. The reading selection was picked out by the barber's son, and plenty of them were about architecture and art appreciation.

"I'll do it," said Jed. "Sure would. Nothing better to do than fall into a bucket at the fair. I was checking out the show last year. The most confusing show I ever saw." This suddenly made Theo perk up, with increasing curiosity. "But the crowd," the hunter reminisced. "They saw the show and it was grand."

"Grand?" Theo asked the hunter.

"You heard what I said, fella," jabbed Jed. He casually described the scene: "Every moment had the crowd pumping. And the women dancing had the men's blood pumping." He smiled and closed his eyes. "Try to imagine . . . skirts shorter than your jacket."

"Sounds like Jed had himself a time," said the barber who had to pause cutting Jed's hair.

"Yes, sir," said Jed. "I peered out and watched the show from the dunking booth. No crowd left at the booth when the magic show started. I was glad when those strong-armed fair goers finally left my silly ass alone. I saw that money in the jar, and I went to watch those heels kicking up dust from the big top tent."

Theo noted how Brewer was being polite when he told Jed his idea was alright, and the withered old Brewer ended the conversation, saying contemplatively, "Maybe we will, alright? Maybe we will have to see what Virgil wants to do. Maybe we'll . . . have a . . . go at the fair next year. We'll have to see. It'll be alright. I . . . bet it will."

"Are you a betting man?" inquired Theodore Bryant.

"I am not," admitted Brewer, "but I know my boy. And he's running around town. He'll be back to lend a hand. He always does when I need him to."

While Bryant flipped through *Modern Art in the 21st Century,* he was approached by the large man dressed in a white long-sleeve buttoned shirt and blue jeans. Monty Brewer was an older man with a dark grey mustache and light grey hair puffing out on the sides but neatly arranged in an uneven part starting near the middle of his head.

Brewer's dark grey mustache was long enough to sweep his bottom lip, but he needed more to reach the dusty tile floor. He picked up a broom and long-armed dust pan, and said to Theo, "Have you eyes enough to see the hair on the ground but not enough to ask about the window, sonny?"

Bryant kept quiet while Brewer finished sweeping the tufts of hair. From behind the magazine about oils and acrylics, Theo focused on the eyes of the sweeping gentleman as he became closer. He swept, until he stopped and stood there, looming over the investigator.

"Well, do you have anything to say?" asked Monty Brewer.

Bryant didn't break his stare as he placed the magazine aside to snatch up the broom from the sweeper's grasp, and he walked backward to bump into a customer. He excused himself improperly without turning to address the new-comers, but without trouble, he swept the broom back to the inside edge of the doorway's threshold. He pulled the broom along like a hockey stick, in front of him, dragging with it a triangular puck of sharp glass. The glass puck was painted blue on one side and smooth on the other.

The glass rested on the floor for only a moment. After it was inspected by the sweeper, he reclaimed the broom and picked up the sharp triangle of glass with metal forceps. He brought it over to the front counter by the door near the cash register for further illumination.

He pried open the bent drawer of the register. From within he produced a fine jeweler's device that shined bright light about its specimen. With contrition trampled by glee, he said, "Look . . . ." By then, even the new-comer customers were drawn in, as was Bryant. The man took from the register a picture of the shop taken long before the window shattered. He held the black and white photograph proudly for all to see. He pointed with his stubby finger to the glass on the shop in the photograph, and he read what it said:

"This is still the 'Martin Brewer & Son Barbershop,' but my father had taken this photo when I just born. He decided . . . I would take over . . . . And look here. Will you please?" asked the barber. He pointed his stubby finger at the photograph, tapping it again and again. At the tip of a pair of scissors painted on the glass, next to a painting of a comb, a cup, and a razor was the piece of glass that had just been swept up with the rest of the hair that falls to meet the floor.

"That is what you found in your charade, sir," said Monty Brewer, still tapping his stubby finger. His other hand held the sharp piece of glass that was painted with an impression of the adjuster screw that holds together the pinch of a pair of scissors. He held it in the light for everyone to see. He said, "My son loved this painting. Why would he destroy it?" He held it tightly between his thumb and pointer finger, enough for it to cause bleeding.

Outside on the sidewalk, Maynard stewed. He stood in his grey cap and rain boots and stared up at the clouds. "You're going to have to excuse me," he said. "I have business of my own . . . to attend to."

McKindley wanted to know what was on his mind, so he asked him, "Are you open on the weekends? I was thinking about coming by for a rug for my den."

"A den without a rug isn't much of a den," Maynard said. "You need a bearskin, my friend. With that type of rug, you will feel like you can whip the most terrifying beast into shape for your own comfort."

"Beautiful," said McKindley. "I'll come by for one. Set one aside for me."

"Sure thing," said Maynard. "Better yet, I'll send one to you. I'll cover the cost of shipping. Drop it off myself to the station."

"Well," said McKindley, "it's good to know you know where to find us."

"With pleasure," the shopkeeper turned and crossed to his shop.

The other barber working in the shop, who had just been busy with a customer in his chair, stopped working with his customer's face to turn to say: "You didn't have to let me come in today, Mr. Monty. I would have rescheduled. It was only a trim and shave for Jed here . . . . He could have rescheduled."

Jed looked up from his hunting magazine and said, "Speak for yourself, buddy. I have to go see my girly tonight, and the buck I clipped wasn't big enough to impress her the least bit."

"What a life," said his barber.

Theo noticed how the barber's neck seemed to reek of the toil but his hips bent properly without slouching. He admired the barber's posture for a moment before skimming an article in the magazine he held. The ancient magazine was an antique, published in 1960. The particular article written by a Spanish Prince was titled *Queenly and Kingly Activities*. The Spanish Prince had celebrated the birth of his daughter, Esmeralda, by publishing a book detailing what is proper for people to do. Theodore Bryant had some cathartic release. Something came over him while he was studying the pictures of the Royal Spanish Families.

"I bet you wish you had their hair," said Theodore. He showed the picture of the Spanish Prince with his long flowing hair to Jed, who frowned for a moment to imagine it.

"You're damn right," said the hunter.

"You're alright there, Jed," said Monty Brewer to the other barber and to Jed. "You needed to feel better about the way you look, and so did these people. We can do it."

"You mean, I can do it," snipped the other barber as he closed his scissors on a long lock of Jed's hair.

Without saying anything, Bryant and the new customers stood by the register and listened to someone else's explanation of what had been going on. The other barber gave his side of the story when prompted by Jed who asked, "Besides, what happened besides that little window opening up like that?"

The other barber moved nervously and looked over to get an idea of whether he had the permission to enchant his audience. He got a read on the situation being tense, so he got out as much description he could, by saying, "Just trust me and stay out of it, Jed. Mr. Monty dealing with a hardship. You hear?"

"What's that got to do with me not getting my hair and shave done today? If anything, he should want the extra money," said the insensitive customer.

"Okay, *Big Bucks*," chimed in Monty Brewer. The dreary eyes of the owner landed on Sergeant Bryant with zero animosity, and he asked, "Are you getting a shave today?"

"If you want, when I'm done with Jed, Mr. Monty, I'll take a look to see if there's something in the back to cover this window," said the mindful barber. "The draft is damn cold on my ankles."

Jed's feet twitched in leather boots before he sharply said, "Least the cold sends the bugs all back to hell where they belong." The barber turned away from Jed to clean his comb.

"I'd like a haircut, please," requested Bryant.

"Okay. He's busy now, and I . . . don't have what I need, so . . . twenty minutes," said Monty Brewer.

The other barber nodded while flipping through Jed's thin crown. He said, "Less than that." The barber emptied a bottle of blue disinfectant called Barbicide into a glass on the counter built onto the mirrored wall.

"Oh come on," said Bryant. "With stories like you tell, I

want you to do it." A sly smile crept over his boney cheeks.

"Sadly," said Brewer, "I cannot. Not today. You'll have to wait, sir." He tended to his bleeding finger and thumb that had went too long unnoticed. He had to sop up some of the blood with paper towels.

"Are you alright?" asked the patient customer who came in after Theo.

Brewer held the towel tightly and he nodded that he was okay.

"Please," said Bryant. "You have such wonderful stories."

Brewer turned to the new customer and asked what he was there for. But when he returned to Theo, Bryant had his badge held high in the air for all to see. He said to the barber, "I think I'll wait to have a chat with you after all."

The very next day, the same four sergeants who responded at the pier visited the barbershop. Early in the morning the shop it was empty. The only person around was the other barber who had been working on Jed's thinly cropped hair. He was reading another one of the art magazines from the waiting area, but he stood up when the badges arrived.

"Back for another shave?" asked the barber.

"We're here for something else," said Theo.

"Well," said the barber, "I'm sorry, but Mr. Monty ain't around. He's on his way to the pier to see if his son washed up, see if he showed up to paint the sculpture again."

Theo picked up a magazine, swirled his coat and sat in the waiting area as the remaining sergeants took over the leather barber chairs. McKindley, sitting next to the barber's station, prompted the styling artist to tend to his area. He wiped down his instruments and used Barbicide to disinfect them. He treated the straight razor kindly. McKindley watched him prepping in the mirror. He took out his wallet and put money on the table next to the magazines. McKindley motioned for the cape and the barber slid the string under his chin and started taking off McKindley's beard. After a moment the barber frowned his lips tightly and said, "It's on the house." Before McKindley could speak, the barber continued, "Mr. Monty, he seemed very depressed."

"We must have passed him on the way here," said McKindley.

"I'll handle this," said Theo. "Thank you, but he isn't the reason we're here in the first place." He dropped his magazine, popped up from his seat and made his way over toward the door. He took the old photograph from the front counter that Monty Brewer had used to identify the piece of painted glass that Theo had swept up the day before.

"Tell me what you see here," said Theo, brandishing the photograph for the others to inspect. McKindley stayed subdued by the moving Japanese steel blade while the other two leaned forward. Theo pointed at an area in the photograph just beyond the painted window.

"In the reflection?" asked Howie Windhurst. Theo nodded, and Windhurst answered, "It looks like a 'Going Out of Business' sign."

The barber laughed and snorted. Theo asked, "What's so funny, Bob?" The barber said, "That's Maynard's shop. He's been putting a new 'Going Out of Business' sign out each year for forty years."

"Hey," said Gerald Manus, "it looks like he's changing his tune then." He reached the opening out to the street and they all noticed Maynard's shop that had a banner outside. Above the new welcome mat, the banner read: "40 YEARS & GOING STRONG!"

Theo approached the shop with Windhurst while the other two, McKindley and Gerald, stayed back and waited for a signal. Howie unbuttoned his overcoat and knocked on the shop's large wooden door. He said, "Mr. Maynard, it's the police. We want to talk," but there was no answer.

Meanwhile, Theo took a knife to a trash bag in front of Maynard's stoop. He dumped it on the grass to find out what made a rattling sound. When he first lifted the bags, empty spray cans coated in dried splatters of yellow rolled out. The rattling cans were followed by a loud thump and crashing splash of metal, like a strike from a bolt of lightning. The commotion came from behind Maynard's shop.

Sergeant Bryant went to investigate the sound coming

from behind the shop. Windhurst stayed out front while Theo crept around to the ally. He saw a tabby cat, a Scottish Fold, coming from the rear door of Maynard's shop that was left open. He thought about walking in, but there was too much ground for one man to search by himself. That's when he locked eyes with Maynard himself coming out from the shadows of his shop.

Mr. Spruce was as grand and mighty in size as a bear cub, and Alfansio Maynard certainly seemed to care for him with the affection only a Papa Bear would have for his cub. He took the cat by its scruff, with one hand, and he told Theo how Mr. Spruce didn't mind being lifted that way. The cat's eyes bulged beneath his tiny folded ears and it let out a soft meow. "These creatures have such elastic pelts. Anyway, I'm sure you have business elsewhere. Sorry Mr. Spruce got you all riled up, under your skin, so to say."

Maynard placed Mr. Spruce down, and the cat hunkered low, as its owner waved at Bryant to follow him over to his shop. The shopkeeper started kicking and pushing the large door to get it to slide on the track it hung upon. As they worked together to slide the door, Theodore noted the strange contraptions in the back of Maynard's shop were unlike those on sale in the front of the store. There were swirling lights, and light-emitting screens. Stacks of liquid-crystal-displays waited to have their pixels colored.

"I saw on the news that there haven't been any developments on finding the young man," said Maynard. After he left the shop door to swing on its own, he walked with Theo. They followed the Scottish Fold out into the alley.

Sergeant Theodore reached down to pet the cat. "What's all that in your store?" inquired Theodore. "You've got some strange things there."

"Those are to sell to arcades," said Maynard. "It looks like Mr. Spruce likes you." The red and black tabby cat purred when Theodore stooped lower to him.

"You're telling me you have a problem with the sculpture and upset about vandals, but you're willing to work with the local arcades?"

"Sure," said Maynard without a shred of uncertainty. "Keeps my business afloat while getting those monkeys off the street.... Back to what I saw, Sergeant. The news reports. Have there been any developments?"

"The news tells everyone what we want it to say," said Theo.

"Why do I find you in my back ally today, sergeant?" asked Maynard.

Theo Bryant stood his ground when he said, "My hair is getting on my nerves, and the barbershop is short staffed, so I thought you might be able to give me a trim."

"Don't be silly," said Maynard. "I don't cut hair here."

"My mistake," said Theo. He carried Mr. Spruce into the back of Maynard's shop and bid the old shopkeeper good-bye before he went away.

Dr. Cynthia Valentico made her way through the main parts of the precinct. She was on her way to her office when Theodore Bryant's voice came through my door.

"They've been having a shouting match about their rival newspapers," said Howie Windhurst, who had been waiting out in the hallway.

"How are you, Mr. Windhurst?" asked Cynthia.

"Fine," said Windhurst.

"Sergeant McKindley," Cynthia greeted McKindley, who stopped in the hall to chat with her.

"Hi, Cynthia," McKindley said. "How do you do?"

"I'm well, and yourself?" inquired Cynthia.

"Thinking about dating again. You have any friends, Dr. V.?"

"Not anyone who would date a guy with a beard like yours," she said.

Windhurst chuckled and McKindley thanked her before continuing on his way.

"I'm sure you'll find one," Cynthia said, sincerely. "Keep looking."

"I'm just tired of flings is all," said McKindley, from down the hall.

"Yep," said Cynthia. "We all are."

From outside my office they could hear Theo butting

heads with me. "I know he's guilty. I just do!" said Theo. "Too bad we have no proof," I said doubtfully.

Cynthia wanted to stay and listen but she figured she would be better off reading what we had to say in print. "Grown men can be so fussy," she said to Howie Windhurst before strutting away.

"I think the spray cans are proof enough to bring Maynard in for questioning," said Theo.

"I don't pay you to think. You can take that to human resources if you have a problem," I told him.

"You don't pay me at all," said Theo. "The city pays me." Theo went over how he picked the spray cans up after they were left in front of his shop.

"I don't know what to tell you," was all I kept repeating.

Meanwhile, as Dr. Valentico crossed the walkway leading to the building attached to the main building, she noted how the traffic was rather listless and felt the cold air coming from the windows. Cynthia untangled one of the tassels tied onto the bottom of her blouse. She adjusted it until it was aligned perfectly to match her ensemble. She entered the Internal Investigations Office. She went straight to her desk, only slowing down briefly to wave at the receptionist as she entered the room.

Later that day, Theodore went to accompany Ross McKindley on following up with the offer he was given on a new rug. Inside Alfansio Maynard's store, the rich old entrepreneur had plenty on display under cases and something rattling around in a cage that he wouldn't let anyone see.

When they first walked into the shop the great big Mr. Spruce came running up the stairs to greet them. Close to his tail was Maynard with a pair of scissors that looked as if they'd seen plenty of action. The shears he held were covered in a blackish-brown grease. A good many cat hairs covered Maynard's hands, but the greasy shears were free of hair. "Gentlemen!" exclaimed Maynard. "I'm surprised you came by, Ross—Sergeant Ross."

"Ross is fine," said McKindley. "And I came by because, when I thought it through, I'd rather you not ship the bearskin."

"Oh," said Maynard. "That's unfortunate. I guess you thought you don't need the thing making all the women's toes curl up . . . ?" He sat the scissors on a red shop towel. Maynard looked at Theo and said, "He can't catch the women like he used to, huh? More for you and me. Are you stepping up next?"

Theo kept quiet, while McKindley said, "Not so. In fact I'd rather have the rug made from a hide. I've got one already drawn up. You know . . . time is of the essence with that."

"Sure," said Maynard. His hands moved around, and the cat hair became free on its own to float around the strange shop. The sight made Theodore back away from the counter towards the door. "Sorry," said Maynard.

"Could I see what rugs you've got for sale?" asked McKindley And if I like those, I was thinking, you can take a commission for the skins I made up. Get them sent to your taxidermist."

"Sounds good," said Maynard, reluctantly. "Great thinking. I'll be with you shortly. Locking the damn cat up from getting out." The shopkeeper chuckled and washed the feline's hair from his palms in a utility sink, before bolting the back door. Maynard made his way to the front door next. The deadbolt clicked loudly, causing Theodore to turn sharply at the sound of metal hitting against wood.

"I usually close up shop when I get into the pelts," said Maynard, and the shopkeeper went about the business of moving some furniture and boxes. McKindley took an ottoman from Maynard's hands and passed it to Bryant. The best rugs were rolled up in the corner of his store, behind a player piano. They were genuine bearskins and elk, patched together with hand woven stitching along the edges.

To present the detail of the rugs, Maynard said, "You'd better use your imagination to see how it will fit in your den." He quickly covered up the glass cases with his bearskin collection. The birdcage behind the counter rattled, and both McKindley and Bryant became interested, but Maynard insisted the birds inside needed privacy during breeding. He showed them a picture of the baby birds from the year earlier. To which Theo said, "Keep that cage closed, or Mr. Spruce might get a little fatter."

Maynard shook his head and said, "He's a gentle guy. Wouldn't hurt a fly. He sits by their cage and looks sweetly inward at the deepest parts of their souls. He'll sit there and stare . . . until the birds are ready to fly free on their own."

Theo had to squat lowly to see the emeralds he marveled over. Maynard brought out the entire collection. Yet, Theodore simply nodded. Everyone could tell he was picturing a woman when he said, "Very nice. Fine to see." He backed away slowly as Maynard put the collection away and went to get some prices for them both.

Looking through appraisal notes and guides seemed to occupy Maynard. That's when Theo attempted to clear up his confusion. He asked McKindley, "I thought you were picking a rug up?"

"No," said McKindley. "Calm yourself, young man. It's called Code Confusion. You hear me?"

Theo nodded but he surely wasn't aware of such an unspoken code. He wrote in his private notes, those for Internal Investigations use only, how McKindley eerily lacked the usual communication skills required of most sergeants, and "for that reason . . . will likely not make lieutenant."

"I'm testing the old man," said McKindley, "to see if he's got any loose ends that we need to snip. He's been acting strange ever since he came into the station." McKindley checked over his shoulder before saying, "Trust my hunch."

"Okay," whispered Theo. "A little heads up next time?"

"Alright," said McKindley. "Listen, I already got the short straw being partnered with a rookie who thinks he can walk over everyone. Doesn't mean I have to take orders from you." He showed his teeth and smiled, to say, "What's wrong? You think you come in . . . and run the place . . . ? Learn to take a knee, Bryant."

"Who are you shopping for?" asked McKindley.

"Nobody," said Theo, "it just caught my eye."

"Right," said McKindley. "You don't have to tell me. I just thought you might be trying to impress the lady who you brought in at the station."

"You're going to have to be more specific," said Theo. "I've brought a lot of ladies to the station."

"Funny," said McKindley. "You know who I mean. The doctor is showing serious interest in your cases."

"That's her job," said Theo.

"Maybe," said McKindley. "She's running Internal because of you. She's pretty. You know . . . . You'd take her out."

"We're professional," said Theo. He smiled a little smile before backing away from the emerald glow.

Maynard was really selling McKindley on the look of the rugs, so he bought a dark colored bearskin, and Maynard went to get some rope to tie the rug up for them to take away.

"Are you always writing?" asked McKindley.

"Not always," said Theodore as he lowered his pad to share with Ross McKindley.

"Why?" asked Ross.

"Details," said Theo, "it's a fancy place, but someone broke into the barbers. That doesn't seem likely."

Their conversation was interrupted when Mr. Spruce knocked over a vase that Alfansio Maynard claimed was worth a month's rent for his shop. Maynard cleaned up the pieces as the cat wandered back down into Maynard's cellar. The Scottish Fold meowed from below them, down the steps. Maynard said he'd need to go feed him after they leave.

Bryant moved to the door and out to the cruiser parked on the street. A few moments passed before McKindley joined him. He passed the time watching the small crowds of people doing their holiday shopping along the strip of stores. People seemed cheerful, and Theo figured plenty of the shops would welcome the business. When McKindley joined him Bryant wasn't expecting the police sergeant would be carrying a rug over his shoulder but he was. He put it in the trunk of the cruiser.

McKindley shifted things around in the trunk while he raved to Bryant about the whole experience in Maynard's shop: "Great, I could have had something, but the Rookie Sergeant and Chief of Internal—How about that, Rookie Sergeant Theodore Bryant? You butchered all my hard work."

"Just take us back to the station," Bryant said smugly.

In the car McKindley tried to smooth things over with his partner, but Theo didn't care about pecking orders, or apologies between coworkers. "You're breaking my concentration," said Theodore.

McKindley snorted and waved him off. "Your concentration . . . ? I'll show you how to concentrate." He took their cruiser up the hill towards the precinct, asking Theo, "You want to know how I concentrate?" The cruiser picked up in speed and they even got a little air when the body of the car shifted on its suspension while coming up over the hill. It landed hard on the cobblestone. It was a rough landing, but skidding to the right near parked cars was worse. That was before McKindley really hit the gas to the floor. "You ever been this fast before?" he asked and he jammed on the sirens to clear the streets.

Theodore laughed and looked at the speedometer. "Nope."

Cynthia was halfway through her day's deliberations. She rested her case book down on the ledge she uses for reading and opened it. She leaned in to examine the profile of a staunch Italian immigrant . . . who was in line to be hired. She was nearly settled into making the call on whether or not to continue the hiring process for the potential new recruit when Theo pushed his chair up to her desk and said, "Got time for tea, Doc?"

"Sure do," said Cynthia, and she closed the case file.

Theo poured hot water from the coffee machine into each mug, and soon, the colorful aroma of last night's mopped floors would be masked by the sudden infusion of English Breakfast. He brought her a copy of the paper he wrote, a dissertation on his findings he jovially dubbed *The Maple Crusader*, and her eyes lead the way into understanding what his past few hours of contemplation . . . had brought him to pronounce to anyone who would read the paper, or talk to him about the case. He believed Maynard was quite guilty, and he vowed to find a way to show everyone the truth in the matter of Virgil Brewer's disappearance.

He sat across from her and meditated over the steaming contents of his mug.

"Still working on finding that barber's son, huh?" asked Cynthia.

"Yes," said Theo, "but I had a break."

"Oh? What is it?" asked Cynthia. He raised his mug and said, "*This* is some kind of break, I suppose." She smiled and said, "I suppose you're right."

"I have a good reason to suspect," said Theo, "the old shopkeeper that lives next—or across the way . . . from the barber. How is your intake process going?"

"Great," said Cynthia. "I'm keeping closed up here in my office. I'm as quiet as I can be while this applicant talks to a series of forms and makes personal voice recordings."

"Well," said Theo, "they never said you had to be personal at work."

"That's right," said Cynthia. "It's a professional's choice as to . . . how close to allow . . . a patient."

"Perfect," said Theo. "And the patients—how are they?"

She rolled her eyes and said, "Not important."

"Sure it is," said Theo.

"No," said Cynthia. "They're tough nuts to crack. And some . . . are tougher than others." She lifted the folder she had been studying earlier, and she said, "This guy has been on parole, but he's been reformed. How do I know he's actually reformed?"

Theo picked up the file for Applicant #42885-1. He looked it over and said, "Yeesh."

"Yes," said Cynthia.

As he read through the case file, he looked up to notice her blue emerald necklace, and something took over him. She could tell it was something she did by the way he smiled and adjusted his glances. She covered her neckline and he lowered her case file.

Cynthia smiled at him. She took her case file back and commented, "So . . . you think it's the old man . . . Maynard . . . ?" Theo nodded. Cynthia asked, "The one who came in here?" He nodded again. "The one who brought the case . . . to us . . . ?" He nodded once more. "Why?" asked Cynthia.

"I think he brought it to us because he thought it would clear his name of suspicions," said Theo. "To be on the right side of the law . . . . And there's the matter of the neighborhood. His lease runs up soon, and the owner of the building Maynard rents has already expressed interest in demolishing the place."

"He's attached to the neighborhood," said Cynthia. "How sad to have such . . . attachments. But I get that. Yet . . . I don't get why you're so sure you have something on him."

"Right," said Theo reluctantly. "Well, not much cash was there to be stolen. Just that beautiful glass mural . . . a piece of history destroyed. No cameras . . . to see who did it. But I found the cans of spray paint in Maynard's trash can. You think that would help."

"Well," said Cynthia, "apparently the captain doesn't think that's enough. What else?"

Theo sipped his tea. He rose up and stretched his arms above his body momentarily before backing out of her small office. He came back for his chair and said, "Good luck on the intake. I'm better off going for a walk . . . I guess."

"Thanks," said Cynthia. "You're a lot of help yourself. I'll have to recommend that this guy . . . . Well, that he gets a haircut for starters." She wrote, on his application, "Appearance this drab?"

"A haircut?" asked Theo. He imagined the magazine he had been reading, and he thought for a moment about what Prince Ascubar, the Spanish Prince with his long flowing mane of hair coming from his head, would have done. "You're brilliant," Theo said to Valentico. He dashed out.

"And you're not bad yourself," called Cynthia after Theodore. After he left, she let her hair out of the bun, uncovered her neckline and resumed her deliberations.

The next day the streets were flooded with traffic since it was rumored that a young prince would appear on his way to the airport. His limousine driver diverted from its predetermined course when he saw the lovely cobblestones that lead to the main street. The limousine parked so that the prince, in his lovely silk robes, could take to the sidewalk on his sandaled feet.

His jewels and rings weighing on his arms brought glimmering reflections to the cement and cobblestones. He stopped in the square and stood in the public courtyard, long enough for a crowd to gather. He made the following decree:

"My appearance as such, in a town such as this, means I will bring my fortune to it in a way of remembrance. Who, I say, whom . . . . Though I suppose I should say . . . . Which of you merchants . . . will cut from my hair to commemorate this occasion?"

His eyes searched until they fell upon the barbershop in ruins.

He wept, and said, "I must ask. The worst store on the block still must have a decent offering . . . in order for royalty to invest . . . in buying this strip, preserving, and expanding all ways of life." The crowd had grown but remained silent. "Yet, this poor rubble of a shop has no offering for my simple request?" Murmuring began. "I only ask that someone trim one hair of my head."

But nobody from the barber's shop stepped forward. People from town lined the streets, coming from the shops and the marketplace nearby.

"Who else might have this offering?" asked the prince. "Who is fortunate enough to offer to a prince . . . so that I may return the bounty with gratitude?"

From the crowd came the old shopkeeper, Alfansio Maynard. He leapt forward. "As spry as you are, you must make fine cuts with your blades," said the prince. Maynard smiled and said, "I assure you, good sir, I will try my hand to be steady near your neck." When the prince unraveled his turban Maynard quickly jutted a pair of greasy scissors near the prince's ear. The stainless steel blades were covered in residue of a hair mixed with a thick coat of grease to allow for quick snips. They made a precise cut, but what was cut wasn't typical human hair. No, it was more like hair belonging to a doll. Thick plastic lashes chopped from the wig. But before Maynard could check to see what was below the hair he cut, the prince slapped a handcuff around Maynard's wrist.

Maynard's hand that held the scissors released, and the stainless steel instrument clattered onto the cement sidewalk.

From beneath the silk robes appeared none other than Sergeant Theodore Bryant; his voice called loudly, "Mr. Monty Brewer, thank you for cooperating with this charade and placing your trust in us to find and apprehend this culprit."

Monty Brewer came about the crowd with the other barber by his side. "Why, yes," Brewer said. "But of course."

"Will you please confirm the scissors on the ground to be your own property?" asked Theo.

"Why . . . . Yes," said Monty. "I can confirm." He picked up the pair of greasy scissors and studied them for a moment. "Do you see where they have been engraved?"

"I do not," said Theodore. He placed his wig and turban on the ground. Alfansio Maynard laughed uproariously.

"What a charade," Maynard said. "You fooled me. Thinking that a prince would come to our crumby street."

"There is an emblem on the scissors with my initials," said Monty Brewer. He looked to the other barber for help.

"Those ugly things," said Maynard. "I use them to cut away matter between Mr. Spruce's paws." The other barber took the scissors from Sergeant Theodore Bryant's hands, and Bob cleaned them off with a blue cleaning liquid. Undoubtedly, the scissors carried a gold emblem on the handle with a capital letter for each of its owner's initials.

McKindley and Gerald took control by taking Alfansio Maynard into the alley alongside his shop as Theodore and Windhurst went into the shop. That's when they found Virgil Brewer kicking around and tied up in the basement.

"I was going to let him out," said Maynard. "I swear I was. He just needed time to think about what he was doing to this neighborhood. That artist ruined the pier, just like the son of the barber is ruining our street. He needed discipline, that boy!"

"You'll have your time for discipline yourself," said Gerald. Sergeant Manus was startled to find Virgil returning willingly into Maynard's shop. The freed young man returned only to take the tabby cat with him.

CASE TWO:

Another true-crime story, as told by L. - Stegner, Captain, the Montréal Police Department.

When you have a few thousand people moving in and out of one space it's easy for certain details to get lost in the shuffle. But when we have break-ins, cars missing, or other red flags that get sent to Internal Investigations . . . things can get a little chaotic.

"Apparently a gun is missing from the ammunitions lock-up," said an intern.

"One gun?" asked Cynthia.

"Yes," said the intern, straightening his paisley collar. "It was a magnum."

"Well," said Cynthia, "if it's just one, try looking behind the shelves then."

When a car goes missing we would normally know about it, unless the car goes missing the same day one of a group of traveling dignitaries disappears. They were on the way through our district to visit a climate change convention when they were taken from the road by force. Their car was hit by another and one of the dignitaries was abruptly taken. They would not make it to the Montréal Climate Control Summit, where one brave engineer would speak to the crowd about his idea to transport a crystal called Elixiumbrium around the globe in order to restart the tides. The moon wasn't pulling the oceans the way it should have been. We anticipated mayhem. Utter mayhem. It was common under times of stress to let simple things like car sign-outs slip away in the pile of demands that matter. Protocol was slipping from our grasp and the department's sense of normality fell apart in a bad way.

Theo had already moved on from being a representative of the Force and working with Internal Investigations . . . to something else entirely. He didn't quite know what he was getting into on his own, but his business was no longer my concern. As long as he didn't break the law or distract Dr. Cynthia Valentico from her consultations for the precinct, he was free to inspect matters on his own. Though I would have sooner bit my tongue in two than give him such permissions.

. . . .

Sergeant Bill Hutchinson drove his police issued, unmarked cruiser near the crime scene, but he made most of the journey on foot that day. He stepped out of the cruiser onto crushed gravel and placed the lone key from the car's ignition into his breast pocket. He walked the rest of the way to secure the crime scene with enough tape around the perimeter to give forensics the room they needed to get to the blood drops on the floor near where the hostage was kept.

DETECTIVE THEO & DOCTOR VALENTICO
IN
BREAD CRUMB TRAILS

HIS LEGS STOPPED BEFORE CROSSING, BUT HIS UPPER BODY MOVED FORWARD TO WHERE THE TRAFFIC WAS STOPPED. Cars lurched forward. He stopped, not wanting to be run down. The driver near the curb saw him there, lunging back and forth with his upper body swaying partially. The drivers completely stopped their motions and waited a second before creeping forward again. Cars in the lane to the east of Theo went, and the gates were open for him to cross. Traffic zoomed through the intersection at full speed.

Theo watched his hefty ex-partner leading a search across the street and tipped his hat to say hello to McKindley. But the newly promoted lieutenant didn't notice; he was busy leading a few of the rookie police on a chase for the visiting member of a royal family: "Let's say he went this way," said McKindley. There were a few other groups moving about the street with the same purpose in mind; Theo knew who everyone was, but he wasn't as familiar with any of the other members of the party. Still, they would know his name because each and every one of those badges paid attention to his paper, renamed *The Street Crusader*. He wrote in it about the latest cases he couldn't cover on his own. In fact, it was Theo's neatly typed and formatted paper that brought about the commencement of the largest manhunt in the history of our Québec Province.

Detective Bryant moved across the intersection alongside the car that waited for him. When the light changed, that driver gave their gas pedal more attention, causing the white hatch-back to drive off quickly. It neared the end of the next block at the same time that Detective Bryant took his first step on the curb. He walked alone, but his trench coat made up for it. The coat took up an equal amount of space on its path as a single unit of two or three rookie police.

When Theo stopped to observe the traffic passing on his right, the jacket clung to him. He moved forward at once, at a quick speed, his gate wider than before. He dashed towards the next intersection. As the corners of his trench coat floated out, he held onto his floppy-eared, deer-stalker hat with one hand.

The crime scene was already roped off with yellow tape when PI Bryant made his arrival. When he stepped under the yellow tape, he unbuttoned his long, pin-striped coat in one motion. Its three buttons opened enough to allow room for his hand to tuck his hat into the inside breast pocket in exchange for a small, wired notepad. He flipped the notepad open along its top coil, and as it hinged open he started to accomplish writing his Introductory Dossier, preliminary notes he would write before speaking to a badge-wearing member of the police department, on the scene.

He wrote in the notepad: "The day is Wednesday and . . . we have secured the crime scene." He wrote the full date underneath that, and he wrote the address: "615 N. Carlyle." He stopped his pen from proceeding further, and he listened for a moment before he wrote, "The time is 10:15, no buzz."

With bulging eyes and words wet with spit, he was approached by such a member of the police department dressed in uniform. The two stripes on the shoulder of his jacket indicated his rank. The sergeant said, "Sir, this is a private party."

"I know that. It's why I'm here," said Theodore, and he extended his boney right hand with its thumb raised high to make for a proper greeting.

"Well," said the tense sergeant, "you're not on the guest list. Scram."

"Negative," said Theodore, and he withdrew his hand. "I needn't provide any explanation to match your hostility, do I?"

"Who do you think you are?" asked the sergeant. He studied PI Bryant's clothing carefully.

Another member of the police department appeared; it was McKindley, who had made lieutenant, rounding the corner of the interior hall with blue latex covering his hands.

Theodore waltzed over to McKindley and said, "What do you make of everything?" He spoke in one long puff.

"Sergeant Hutchinson, you can relax," said McKindley to the aggressive cop. "He's here to cause trouble. I know it," said Hutchinson. "No Bill, let him in," said McKindley to the fierce Sergeant Hutchinson. Bill Hutchinson decided to leave them and go attend to straightening the yellow-taped barrier. "Thank you for joining the investigation, Bryant."

"Sergeant Theodore Bryant. Oh, sure. Right. Private detective, I forgot. It's been awhile," said McKindley.

"Ross," said Theodore. "Are you well?"

"I am," said the tired eyed McKindley.

"Last time I saw you," said Theo, "weren't you looking for a taxidermist?"

"Hell of a memory, Theo," said McKindley. He was plump with nostalgia. "Heck of a time we had. You're a whip." He looked to the angry sergeant. "Bill Hutchinson's a sergeant still. You remember Bill?"

"I don't think we met," said Theo.

"Yeah," said McKindley, "still not promoted up the ladder like myself. So he wouldn't get it."

"Get what?" asked Bill.

"Theo here," said McKindley, "used to let him drive my whip."

"You did?" asked Bill.

"No," said McKindley, "but I would have."

"Do you mind?" asked Theo.

"Generally, no," said McKindley. "I don't mind, but Bill does. Do you mind, Bill?"

Bill grunted, but Bryant had heard enough. He continued to the scene on his own until McKindley followed suit.

In the adjacent room, Theodore cut right to it: "Now, bring me up to speed with your notes, or else I'll be forced to call the newspaper to compare notes with them," said Bryant, as a reporter flashed his press badge to the suddenly standoffish Sergeant Hutchinson. Despite having laminated credentials, the press was denied entry but kept with the spirit of journalism by taking plenty of photographs of the crime scene from behind the tape.

"Thanks, now Bill Hutchinson is going to be hitting around my taxidermist . . . when I like to keep him busy all year," said McKindley when they were on their own.

"Not my fault," said Theo.

"You're funny, Detective," said McKindley. "How you're not afraid to leave it up to the police for once. Calling us in as your back up, huh? We got your message and I personally responded to the report you dropped off."

"Thank you, lieutenant," said Theo. "I needed to see my loves before I got any deeper here. Closer to the action."

"I understand. I wish I understood better frankly," said McKindley. "What you and Valentico have. No man should come between it. The way you look at her, he'd have to be an idiot or lunatic or—You ever have any trouble keeping her?" Ross winked at Theo.

"I'm busy, lieutenant, but I appreciate your friendly banter," said Theo. "I do—just time is of the essence. Let's get to the dignitary before anything goes wrong. Finding Lady Raindaleigh. Let's get to finding her."

"The dignitary," admitted McKindley. "Right. Important person. I know."

"Not just that," said Theo. He drew his bottom lip in before saying, "There's a connection to something greater, you see. But, I can't talk about that now. Let's get to the search."

As the press reporter blinded Hutchinson with the camera's flash mechanisms, the light bounced around in the hall and seemed to jolt Bryant into an urgent search. And the reporter asked Hutchinson about the case: "I want to know, sir, is there any update on the kidnapping of Lady Raindaleigh?"

The reporter was the first of many to show up at the scene that day, since the story had somehow made it to the public already. But Hutchinson was prepared; he said, "No comment for the press at this time," while clenching his leather-gloved fists.

Of course, McKindley knew of Bryant and remembered him from their time together before Theodore left the Force. He had a hunch that Bryant would show up to the case on his own accord.

There are a number of factors that determine how quickly a case will turn cold. One of the main factors is human traffic. The more the police search the scene, the harder it is to find the trail of a warm body, even if the person searching is a professional. Too often does the trail get cold and the warm body of the kidnap victim resides permanently at a destination unknown. In this particular case, the private investigator arrived on the scene just after the first responding members of the police department; all the people Bryant saw on his way to the scene were patrolling the surrounding community. Bryant was the third person on the scene at N. Carlyle.

McKindley checked for prints on the door knobs and all the obvious places when he first arrived. Bryant didn't bother with those types of procedures when the police were already on the scene, which is one of the main reasons he invited them.

"I'll let you know, Bryant, if we need you for any outside assistance," said McKindley.

"Do you ever stop talking?" asked Bryant, and he said, "You'll find silence to be golden." Just then, the air conditioner clicked on, prompting Theo to ask if it was running the entire time.

McKindley straightened up and listened to the machine buzzing and blowing. He said, "I believe so, Bryant. I haven't touched it. I'll check with Hutchinson." Then, McKindley stepped away.

Theo moved toward the wall. He listened intensely. He noticed a white substance on the floor and looked closely at it. He found the substance to be a small amount of bread crumbs. McKindley returned to watch Theo follow the wall to the corner of the room, passing a closet where the vent for the central air system was located, next to a book shelf. He took a pen from his pocket as he knelt down near the corner of the room, where the air was being sucked away from the rest of the space. He retrieved a small corner of plastic wrapping, balancing it on the tip of his pen. He extended it for Lead Investigator McKindley to take in with his eyes.

McKindley found the rest of the cracker packet in a ball, dancing in the wind. He picked it up and kept moving with Bryant. There was a good amount of mud at the end of the road near the woods behind the industrial park where they started their exterior investigations. It looked like someone had ran through it. Theodore walked around the perimeter, noticing a large square heel imprint on the shallow bank of a puddle. Next to the shallow bank were tracks indicating someone or something was dragged to the woods.

They didn't enter the woods because Bryant spotted something suspicious on the edge of the wooded area. There was a sticker bush that looked like it was recently plowed down by a person and whatever they had dragged through it.

The victim was last seen wearing a grey hooded sweatshirt. Grey cotton fibers were stuck on the sticker bush. A long, nylon thread stood out to Bryant in the prickly thicket, so he plucked the thread loose and studied it. The tracks indicated the action was moving westward. It appeared that the perpetrator cut through the thorns instead of going into the clearing behind the industrial park. McKindley said, "They did it to lose the trail. Do you think?" Theo responded, "No. Something isn't right. Let's go around."

Bryant yelled for a taxi, and they climbed aboard an old yellow cab.

The cab drove around the block to the other side of the woods where a fountain existed among benches.

"It was raining last night."

"Look. There's prints— The footsteps lead to the corner."

From the fence near the fountain and benches, the kidnapper must have dragged their prize to a car waiting by that corner.

"They must have an accomplice . . . in on it with them."

Theodore Bryant carefully followed the tracks, crouching down over them with bent knees and clunky footsteps. The tracks diverted near the benches.

"It looks like the kidnapper paused," said McKindley.

"Yes, but you say it was raining?" asked Bryant. He stepped lively along the path of drips on the pavement to the trashcan where he poked his head in to investigate.

PI Bryant lifted from the garbage can a grey nylon hooded sweatshirt, soaked and splattered with mud and some other substance on it. The stain was near the collar. The detective smelled the shirt and nodded, and he took from his pocket the nylon string removed from the bush of thorns. The string matched perfectly with the fibers that composed the shirt found in the garbage at the park. He turned the messy shirt over to reveal a jagged edge where it tore on some thorns.

"It looks like someone . . . romped through the mud and wanted to lose their wet clothing . . . before they hopped in with a friend."

"Yes. It appears that way," added Bryant. "But they may have done better if they bought their lunch at the deli, however."

"I don't follow you," said McKindley.

"You will. No time to explain," said Bryant. "Meet me at the crime scene. I have to make a stop some place."

Theo stood outside the metropolitan's largest subway station, where Cynthia stood with him waiting for her train.

"You think you can track down where it's from?" asked Cynthia.

"Well, I'm not exactly a blood hound," said Theo.

"Right," said Cynthia. "Well, you ought to look around . . . You know, the criminals are just people . . . . People have to buy their food somewhere. Maybe some deals at grocery stores . . . ?"

"That's an idea," said Theo.

Cynthia said, "You found what you think is peanut-butter—"

"I know it's peanut-butter," says Theo, "because peanut-butter has the most distinct smell of all the smells."

"That's not entirely true," said Cynthia. "It could have been chocolate, or anything else on that shirt. You found it in the garbage can in a park, so for all anyone knows it could have been already in the garbage can."

"I know peanut-butter when I smell it," said Theo. "You usually have a way of kicking me in the right direction. Can you think of anything?"

"I think," said Cynthia, "you must be very hungry, dear." She got on her train, and Theo stood there a few moments by himself.

Along came this tall man who was walking along the sidewalk near the platform in casual attire with thin glasses and bald head. He was using an old flip-phone but he wasn't ashamed:

"Take a look out for it next fall, man. Yeah .... Is-is that who I think it is ...? Hold on. Alfred ...?" he said to a man who just got off the train car.

"Yeah," said Alfred. "Who you talkin' to?"

"It's Fred," said the man.

"I remember Fred," said Alfred.

"How you know Fred?" asked the man. "—Hey Fred, listen. I'm with Alfred. I'll give you a call back, man."

"I remember him," said Alfred. "How you been bro?"

"I'm good," said the man. "You . . . on your way to work?"

"Yep," said Alfred. He took off his bright yellow vest and held it in one hand, "I got to get there. I've been collecting scrap metal, right . . . ?"

"Right—"

"Well, Choy had me out," said Alfred, "brought in my big ol' truck, left up to the scrap yard in Merdeville. I just came back $1,500 in my hand, and Choy so happy he gives me hugs. He's hugging me and thanking me . . . ."

"That's great, Al," said the man. "Are you still with the missis?"

"Yeah," said Alfred. "But we got a divorce."

"Oh no!" exclaimed the man.

"Yep," said Alfred. "Her choice, but it's all right. She found guys not treating her so good after me, and I couldn't find no one better than her. So we back together now."

"Uh-huh—"

"We knew it wasn't right," said Alfred. "Yeah .... Matter of fact, we fell asleep in each other's arms the night we got the divorce."

"Well, too bad they don't have divorce annulments," said the man.

"Huh?" asked Alfred.

"You get married too quick you get an annulment," explained the man, "so you aren't married anymore, but what happens if you get divorced in too much of a hurry?"

"Huh," thought Alfred. "Yeah. Well, this is my train." He got on and walked along to find his seat. "Tell Fred I say 'Hi,' alright?"

"Oh— I will!" exclaimed the man.

"Alright," said Alfred, and his train got down the tracks. He didn't get far before a man with a badge came up on him.

The badge said, "Good evening, sir. I'm with the police department. We're interviewing all the folks who were out on site Thursday night." He looked at Alfred's yellow vest and hard hat. "This is an official police investigation. Follow me."

They stepped off the train at the next stop and rode in a squad car to get back to the place where the kidnapper was held. They got out of the car and into a trailer parked next to a construction site. McKindley was seated behind a desk. Blueprints were rolled up to make room for McKindley's clipboard and notes.

After the police made their introductions, they left room for Alfred to speak. Alfred said, "I had moved . . . to another shift. I wasn't there."

"You mean to say . . . you weren't here on Thursday night?" asked McKindley.

"Well," said Alfred, "they had me pouring mix that morning."

"I don't follow," interrupts Theo who stepped forward from the back of the trailer, where the darkness of surrounding boxes blended with the color of his khakis to mask his presence. He said, "You were pouring mix? For . . . ?" He scratched his head and searched within himself briefly, garnering much attention from the others. "Are you saying . . . you're a baker on the side . . . ?"

"What?" asked Alfred.

"I mean," said Theo with a serious tone, "where do you . . . find all the time?"

"No. I mean . . . . Pouring mix for concrete, Jack'o!" said Alfred with a shake of his head.

"Oh . . . ?" said Theo.

"Okay. Please go on," said McKindley.

"They moved the job around. Sorry. I wasn't anywhere near the warehouse come nightfall," said Alfred.

"Will you show us what concrete you're talking about?" asked the sincere McKindley.

Alfred nodded and got up to go to the door. Sergeant Gerald Manus and Howie Windhurst (who had been appointed as Chief Inspector just recently) were there already to escort him out.

Outside the warehouse, Alfred stopped walking and said, "So here. This is where we poured it." There was an enormous boot print, and a mark that looked like a person was dragged. Two high-heels were in the concrete, drying in the sun.

McKindley's eyebrow was firmly raised when he turned to square-off with Theodore Bryant, to say: "Ex-detective Bryant—" Bryant interrupted, "You mean, ex-cop." McKindley continued, "Yes. I know what I said. I think . . . they went . . . this a-way."

Theo said, "I'll go check to see if we know the victim's shoe size to confirm if it's really our mark," and he left the scene.

By that time, I was at my cruiser already. I took an unmarked cruiser at the station to get to the warehouse since my regular ride was in the mechanic's shop. I signed out the car with a scribble on the yellow pad, before taking the keys for it and popping them onto my quick release chain.

When I pulled the car up to the crime scene, I drove around to where I heard the shots being fired, but on my way around, I put in a call: "Send an ambulance. We got a civilian wounded." I passed Alfred holding his shoulder and moving quickly to get behind my car.

"You'll be alright," I said before performing basic first aid to wrap the wound and stop it from bleeding heavily.

The shots came from behind Bill Hutchinson's cruiser. Bill must've heard the group at the cement print and knew it was only a short amount of time before they were onto him, and he didn't want to be taken down like that. So he fired a few rounds, one of which winged Alfred. PI Theo Bryant ducked behind a dumpster, with McKindley returning fire.

"No. Bill. What did you—" McKindley said with shock.

"You had a part in this, did you?!" Theodore shouted out at Bill.

"I would be lying and the villain of your paper if I told you otherwise. I did it for the bottom dollar they're paying me!" shouted Bill Hutchinson from behind a corner of the brick building. He continued firing upon them.

"Who's paying you?" asked Theodore while hiding from the gunfire with McKindley.

"He's got a couple of us . . . on the bill. Not just me," said Hutchinson. "You know who—The Duke's uncle. He's rich. The whole Drake Family is loaded—" From the sound of the heavy fire, Theodore could tell that Bill was out and needed to reload.

Bryant came out from behind the dumpster to say, "They didn't want it to go down at the convention—so they hired you to keep Lady Raindaleigh—to . . . ." McKindley pulled Theodore away from being a sitting duck out in the open, before Bill Hutchinson could throw more bullets their way. "I've got to get to the convention," said Bryant to McKindley.

"Cover your ears, and shut your mouth," said McKindley to Theo before returning fire from behind the dumpster.

"You're wasting your time," said Bill.

McKindley shouted at Bill, "No— Bill, tell us why you were hired!"

"I'd rather end your publication!" shouted Bill.

"He's pinned us here as a distraction," said Theodore to McKindley.

"From what? What does he have to distract us from?" asked McKindley. "Sounds like he's a bit peeved about your paper. Subscribe to this," said McKindley before barreling out from the dumpster with his rifle held tight to his side.

"He's keeping us from whatever is happening at the convention," said Theodore.

That was where they were when I snuck up on Hutchinson with a stun gun. The diodes were in mid-air when Bill Hutchinson caught them, so I couldn't shock him. Bill whipped that electric wire around the handle of my stun gun, yanking it to the ground and breaking it into several pieces upon impact. What a sight to see, just before McKindley fired a bullet into the back of Bill Hutchinson's head.

Hutchinson fell to the ground and let out a loud gurgling sound. We heard a pounding coming from inside the cruiser, so I held a handkerchief in my hand as I searched for a key to unlock the car and open its trunk.

"I'm thinking of adding an obituary to *The Crusader*," said Theodore in a solemn tone, as he joined me to examine Bill's lifeless corpse.

"McKindley already gave you your first entry," I said in a tone of disgust for the fallen officer.

"You know you're going to have to bring the Duke in for questioning," said Theo.

"Good luck," I said as I searched for the key to unlock Hutchinson's cruiser. "Nobody has seen Duke Framingham since he left on a party cruise bound for Cook Island."

"The Cook Islands are halfway around the planet," replied Theo.

"That was six months ago, too."

"The Duke could be anywhere then," admitted Theo. "He's been running ever since his fiancé died."

I found the key in Bill's breast pocket where he placed it securely that morning upon his arrival on the scene. I went to unlock the trunk but the key wouldn't open it. "I can hear someone," I said with my ear pressed near where the trunk closed to meet the license plate.

Theo said, "That key?" To which I said, "It opened the car but won't open the trunk." Theo looked at the key in my hand and said, "When you check out a car they give you two keys. One of those keys does everything—opens the trunk, door, and glove box, and starts the machine—"

Cautiously, McKindley stepped behind the dumpster and crept down the hill near the river.

I held Hutchinson's key high enough for Theo to examine it. He said, "Yep." I asked Theo, "You said one key does everything. What about the other key?"

39

"That's the valet key!" exclaimed Theo. "It only opens the door . . . and starts the engine. There's another key . . . for the trunk."

McKindley urgently tromped from the river up the hill to meet us at the cruiser. He stepped over Bill Hutchinson and said, "Sorry, mate." He came close to the trunk and said, "Look what I found . . . glistening in the sun down by the river!"

McKindley helped open the trunk, stopping me from prying at it . . . with my bare hands. The hostage was alive and only suffered a few minor injuries, cuts and bruising.

I told McKindley, "Thank you for stepping in."

"You wouldn't have done it without me," Theo said to McKindley with a gloating exasperation.

Back at the station, I reviewed the video footage . . . to see who signed out Bill's squad car. But it wasn't Bill Hutchinson on the tape; it was a much heftier man in a scarf, grey nylon hooded sweatshirt, and hat hiding his face.

"Looks like we have a problem," were the words coming out of my mouth, as McKindley entered my office.

"Problem?" asked McKindley. "I don't want a problem."

I didn't want to scare him off from the case and I had to figure out what I was going to tell the press about the incident at the convention, so I told him, "Me neither, but sometimes problems . . . track you anywhere you go."

Later on, Theodore recounted the events to his wife in a private therapy session she designed for her husband. She told him a little about her experiences with a member of the Drake Family: "The last time I saw the Duke, one of the only times I saw him, he came to me right after you and I met. When I was in the hospital with bits of me the doctors had just stitched up. Nobody came to see me except you and the Duke. He was singing and drunk, I think. He scared me. I thought he was going to get his revenge right then and there."

"Do you think he'd have some reason to be involved in the kidnapping?" asked Theo.

"He was torn up about losing her," she recalled. "When he lost his fiancé. He was singing about her. That was sincere. Psychopathic, perhaps. But he was heartbroken. I don't think he has the motive to be involved in hiring your kidnapper though. Do you think the Goose could have contacted him?"
"Anything is possible," said Theo. "Eugenio Drake, a.k.a. the Goose, was in his deli in Never York when he found out the hostage was released. Someone had distracted the cops around here enough. Security at the convention was low. The summit on climate change. There weren't any police left near the convention center to respond to the attack."
"How are you after all that, Theo?" asked Cynthia. "You didn't know it was happening. It wasn't your fault you weren't there to stop it."
"Shots rang out and I could hear them from where we were," said Theo. "We had . . . freed the captive dignitary . . . ." Theo had rushed to the scene in Valentico's sedan, and it was a good thing she kept it gassed up, as he took the highway, and it was quite a few miles before he reached the convention center.

As they waited for me to return to my office, Theo wrote notes in his dossier: "Some tough old guy knew to wear Kevlar thick enough to resist an armor piercing round. He said it's something he tested out in the war and it once absorbed shrapnel at close range."
I came in after briefing the press about what happened at the convention.
"You lied to them, right Stegner?" asked Theo.
"I told them what they needed to hear," I said.
"Which was a lie," said Theo.
"If anyone is after the old man at the convention, they should think he's dead," I said.
"Exactly," said Theo, "you lied to them. Good job, Captain."
"Where is he now?" asked Cynthia.
"He left on the balloon," I replied.
"That man needs some boundaries," said Cynthia.
"They went back home to Never York. They're the people who are going to fix this mess with the tides. I got to tell you both something, but it's not my jurisdiction."

"What?" asked Theo.

"My . . . . I have no say in it . . . . But if we let something get in the way . . . . The Oriel Family are very important to the . . . to our survival. They're restarting the tides."

"They're restarting the tides . . . ?" asked Theo.

"Yes," I said. "The tides have slowed down without much notice to most people, but something to do with the moon and its gravitational pull. I don't know the specifics just yet, but the old man has a strange crystal to fix it all."

"They're restarting the tides . . . ?" asked Cynthia.

"They're restarting the tides!" shouted Theo.

"Elixiumbrium!" I declared. "That's what it is, the crystal the old man has, I mean."

"I see," said Theo.

"Do whatever it takes, you two," I advised them. "Go to the ends of the Earth to make it so."

"You're serious!" shouted Cynthia in disbelief.

"Take what you want from here," I said. "The cameras are off for Theo and Valentico." I held out a key. I even handed it to Theo who put it in his wallet to be used when the time was right . . . . When the world would need the husband and wife duo to spring into action.

CASE THREE:

One night Theo's old pal from back when he was young, who studied with him before the academy, caught up with him. While they waited for the rain to stop they layered on lunchtime items in a little Sicilian-Italian restaurant. They were over by Mont Royal, where the offbeat crowd would normally gather. They planned to gawk at artsy people and smell the hookah coals, and it's debatable as to who said what after the third course to start the drinks, but they promised their appetites would come in handy when the server wouldn't return with their last round of licorice schnapps. He thought they had too many, and he was right.

What followed was the use of bottled spirits to aid in the delivery of emotions. After he told his friend all about his longings for a woman who had expressed interest in him, he got a cab to take him and his friend to another place that was owned by his bookie, Andrew's Divebar off Main St., where all the party busses lined up. And she was there, standing and looking for a seat. Cynthia never had a chance.

His friend from school had enough to drink to leave in a hurry with a woman that carried him back to her home. It was all the friend had talked about: "Catching some tail near Mont Royal," he kept saying to Theo all night, so Theodore didn't wake him from his friend's drunken haze to tell him that Bette wasn't as beautiful as his friend had imagined. His friend was watching the way she held a beer bottle and left with her in a hurry.

Eventually Theodore found his way over to talk to her. He found the perfect opportunity to move across the bar when Earl started calling after Cynthia. Earl, the old railroad tycoon many people called 'Tater', was harmless, but Theo thought he'd do the gentlemanly thing by arriving on the barstool between them. He saved her from Earl's toothless grins and bourbon breath. They both knew Earl loved to corner women and call them sweetie.

Theo could tell Cynthia would be easy to win over since her eyes wouldn't come off him when he sat down across from her at the bar. When they started talking he knew they were finding a connection. The corner of his badge meant Earl would take off. There were no surprise questions for her to follow up with this time.

She leaned in to say, "I've seen one of those up close before."

"Are you a bad girl—" flirted Theo. A self-aware shock that he said what he said came over him at that moment.

"Yes," said Cynthia, "but the police will see it another way. You know you could have gotten a rise out of me if I was running from you and your department." She dropped the shot back and down came the glass on the bar with a '*Slam!*'

"That means less on me than what you have got as a problem with my team," slurred Theo. "You lump all—everyone with a badge in the same category of nut job."

"Let's be clear, Theo. You fall into a category that is all your own," said Cynthia. "Your symptoms are common, but," she stopped talking and longed for him to catch up with what she was saying.

"My symptoms ...?" said Theo. "When you start caring about my symptoms outside of the precinct, well, then we'll see what happens." The bartender bought them drinks, as old Earl napped in the corner of the crowded bar.

DETECTIVE THEO & DOCTOR VALENTICO
IN
A DAY AT THE FAIR SPARKS INTRIGRUE

44

"WHAT ARE YOU DOING THIS EVENING?" asked an intern to another intern. The office was full of them. Although they were making the place run smoothly, Valentico was tired of listening to their cooing speech.

"I haven't got any plans yet. Still setting things up at my new place," said the other intern. "Why do you ask?"

"—You should check out the fair when you get a chance," said the first intern. "It's only here . . . until Sunday."

Valentico had been trying to concentrate on reading Theo's latest discourse of *The Crusader*. The latest edition had been written specifically for Internal Investigations. She didn't want to be disturbed.

"I'll think about it," said the other intern, "but I have too much to do . . . for finals."

Overhearing the conversations about boys, getting haircuts, study guides, and other social commentary provided a lonely experience for Cynthia, and she thought to herself how nice it would be to have friendship like theirs at work. She shut her office door, started talking to herself aloud about her loneliness, and counted to herself to find calmness and serenity. As she did this she caught onto a set of negative thought patterns before they got the best of her. She told herself, "Friends are anyone you talk to and identify with as an equal. Strangers can be friends. Anywhere you go there are new friends, and they won't care what condition your ear lobes are in." She let her hair down to cover the scars anyway.

"Hello and welcome to an inquisition grander than any spectacle on the third dimensional plane," barked the ring leader of a show that started under a tent at the fairgrounds in Montréal. Plenty of people gathered around, even paramedics got out of their docked yellow and blue ambulances, to see what the noise was about.

In plain clothes, McKindley was in the crowd watching, among spectators when Jed left his dunking booth to watch the strange show in the company of a massive crowd of spectators. Jed especially watched the women closely. Under the big top tent, there were trumpets playing, a man on high-wire did his routine, and at least twenty acrobats in full-body spandex suits worked tirelessly to mask their faces and form various arrangements.

"It is our inquisition of fright," said the ring leader as the high-wire artist slipped but caught himself! "Fright and mayhem and . . . . He-heh-he . . . . A tale or two of truth . . . or lies. Believe what you must, but whatever you do, don't forget to remember . . . when you wake . . . this was all . . . a dream." And the ring leader, with his top hat tied to keep his chin from falling off, faded away in a fog.

The ring leader reappeared at the back of the room, behind the standing crowd, with his top hat and glasses still intact, and he said, "Hide your eyes if you have a weak heart, and part your hair if you wear a toupee."

The crowd naturally made room around him as he spoke: "And now, I'd like to ask for a volunteer," said the ring leader as he combed the audience with his eyes and gloved hands. He looked for the individual who described himself in the letter . . . in formal attire with a blue pin on his tie. He found him and said, "You, sir! You look like you have some trouble that I could comprehend." The crowd was happy to see any kind of free show; people applauded and laughed.

Certainly, the ambassador from Spain took the stage and gave a wink to the ring leader to signal that he was correct in selecting him from the crowd.

A table selling strange antiques and weavings had a poster for a show later on that caught McKindley's eye. The plain clothes sergeant had been trying to seem interested in the event and trying to fit in as another spectator all afternoon. "Are you in the business?" asked plain clothes McKindley. Ross McKindley unbuttoned his leather jacket to get to his inside pocket.

The person he spoke to that ran the table was wearing a costume of a minstrel with a mesh mask over their face. The minstrel was round from hibernating near the gourmet food vendors all afternoon. The minstrel moved slowly to reach McKindley and jingled their hat when they finally reached him.

"Funny," said Ross, who removed from his inner pocket a watch on chain. He opened the watch, snapped the watch closed again, and placed it in a different pocket altogether. The chain leapt from one pocket to the next. He said, "Now that I fit in, will you talk to me?"

"What do you want to know?" asked the strange minstrel.

A series of dancing girls came out. One line of smiling women kicked their ways across to surround the elevated platform of the stage, creating a barrier between the performers and audience. At that time a stage hand brought out a table and another helper brought out a chair. Soon enough the ring leader was left alone with the ambassador on stage. They sat across from each other, and the purple, velvet cloth rose above the table, shimmered and floated back down when the upward facing wind turbine beneath the stage turned off.

"Tell us," spoke the ring leader loudly, "to what pleasure does a foreign traveler like yourself find the time to visit our shores?"

"Time to spend searching for how happiness exists in places outside my own home, sir," said the ambassador from Spain. "It is worth . . . investigating. Your inquisition knows happiness, do you?"

"I believe your path is crossing ours today for a good reason," said the ring leader loudly to the ambassador and loud enough for the audience to hear. "The fortune you deserve to hear today is that you have come a long way, sir, to find what you have had all along."

"Thank you, sir," said the ambassador to the ring leader. He stood before everyone and emptied the contents of his suitcase, placing a file folder down on the velvet cloth. The dull folder muted the sparkling purple fabric.

Dr. Cynthia Valentico was there at the fair too. She decided to go out and see the town spectacle after all. She noticed the crowd, and she went under the tent to see what was happening. When she saw Theodore with a top hat and stage makeup, she couldn't hold back her squeals of laughter. She laughed so loudly that people wondered what was happening and if she was part of the act. As the crowd turned from the alluring stage reading, the ambassador snuck out from behind the backstage curtain. He delivered the file he promised, he helped avoid an international crisis, and he got off the scene before he was even questioned by police.

Meanwhile, McKindley squatted near the back of the cage and he said, "You're sure it's safe?"

"The old girl is blind," said the minstrel. "As long as you don't move fast. Go slow."

Ross McKindley took off his leather jacket and stood level with the warm pile of furry animal before him. The creature snored and huffed. McKindley stepped close enough for her to swat his pant leg, but she remained still.

"She's not hungry," said the minstrel. "I just fed her."

"I bet she can eat," said McKindley.

"Oh, she can eat, alright," said the minstrel.

After the show was over Theo had a few words with Cynthia about her blowing his cover: "You could have cost us that evidence to stop the smugglers. Thanks to the ambassador, whom I didn't even get to say good-bye to, we were able to track down the arms, but that could have been bad."

"Well, you and the other detectives didn't have a chance to take him in . . . in handcuffs for questioning. Anything else to add?" asked the beautiful doctor.

"You're making my point clear."

"He handed you the key and that wasn't enough."

"I'm grateful he came forward but he might have known more if you didn't blow my cover."

"What if he does know more? He came forward when he could. That's all we can ask of the rest of the world sometimes, Theo."

"He did help us stop the smugglers. That would have been mayhem."

"Utter mayhem!" shouted Cynthia.

"Is that some joke you heard from Stegner? You both had a good laugh, huh?" replied Theo.

She said, "Laughter is a great healer. You should try it, Bryant."

That prompted him to say with a smile, "What a wonderful idea. Do you have any more wonderful ideas, dear?"

She liked being called dear by him and so she said, "Yes, I do." And she kissed him for the first time there in her office. His prosthetic chin landed on her desk, and his top hat fell to the floor. She told the receptionist to cancel her next few patients, that she felt ill, and they took off together for the rest of the day.

It was only a matter of time before Theo talked to Cynthia about the carnage he had seen:

"It's taken a toll on me. The bloodshed. I've decided against field work. I'll do all my work on the computer and dial tone. And I'll even do everyone's paperwork, so if they put me on cases . . . . Well, I'll put myself in as investigator . . . of compiling notes. Look . . . here." He showed her a box of notes. It was an old shoe box with his shoe size still printed on the label, but he had crossed the rest out with a marker. Boxes stacked up along the walls of Bryant's office, for he would use them when he needed to go through the notes.

He used the brown cardboard kind of file boxes with lids that fit when they were available, but he seemed to be running through shoes frequently, or running out of them altogether. Anyway, when he stepped down from running Internal, he had to get rid of the shoe boxes, so he used them to carry personal mementos like the one he showed Cynthia that day.

"I wanted you to have this," he told her when he came into her office. "I've read it already," she said. When she turned to her desk she picked up the paper while saying, "Interesting article," but she noticed the small jewelry box underneath the paper.

"For me?"

"It's my way of saying thank you for all the help, and congratulations, on your promotion."

"It looks very nice," she said and she pulled the string of blue emeralds from the box.

They kept the conversation going but relocated to get out of the station.

"Excuse me," said Theo as he elbowed his way in next to Cynthia at the bar. The pub near the station gets crowded near lunchtime.

"Loosen up, pal," said Cynthia. "We're out and it's just us."

"Okay," said Theo. "But don't tell me to 'loosen up.' Alright. Sorry. I know how it looks. I'll put my badge away."

"That's a good start," said Cynthia. "Now we can talk about what's bothering you. I'm off the clock. It's not hourly. I might claim this was a business dinner though, so order what you want."

After they ate and drank a few, Cynthia got back to talking with Theo about what he had seen in his line of work. "The headaches and anxiety are common," said Cynthia. "I looked into your file. You've had the symptoms for how long?"

"A while," said Theo. He gritted his teeth and smiled at her.

"Your symptoms are typical," said Cynthia, "but your recourse in dealing with them—that's what sets you apart from the average badge."

Theo had respectfully avoided the dancing girls and their illustrious behinds in glittering spandex tights as they went through an elaborate finale with high-kicks and heels together; the crowd was distracted enough to allow for Theo to enter and exit the stage, like a trained magician, during his disappearing act at the fair. By the time he left the stage he made the following articles vanish: a file containing one picture, and one silver key.

The picture was of a locker that the key belonged to, numbered and printed with the Montréal Port Authority's insignia of two silver American Goldfinches. When Theo visited the bus terminal to open the locker he found the station to be pristine, clean, and empty; most of the civil passengers were corralled behind velvet ropes near the front desk and terminal doors. The hallway leading to the lockers was empty, except for a piss-drunk old timer . . . who was fast asleep. He stirred when Theodore passed by him and Theo said, "Keep it down, Tater. It's me."

"Oh," said the old man and he dozed off comfortably on his belongings and cardboard mattress.

Inside the locker was an archive of the weapons cache that was scheduled for shipment and exact details on the next trade.

"Well," said Theo, "it appears we found what we're looking for after all, Miss."

"I'm doing my job as a consultant," said Cynthia, "to advise and oversee your internal operations."

"An internal for our Internal," said Theo casually.

"Yes," said Cynthia, "I do believe so."

"Well," said Theo, "then we will be seeing each other again."

"Yes," said Cynthia. "I suppose."

"Alright," said Theo. He motioned and said, "I'll . . . see myself out."

"Oh Theodore?" asked Cynthia. "I suppose I found what I was looking for after all, as well. This case work, I mean . . . . Running Internal on my own will be a lot of work. Perhaps we should still meet to discuss things."

"Good," said Theo. "I mean, Jolly great."

McKindley was still at the fairgrounds to watch all the vendors packing up their tents and closing up their shops. It was the last day for the fair and plenty of vendors had to move on to make strict deadlines, for the next fair was a few towns over. Sergeant McKindley was able to spend more time with the minstrel before the cage was loaded onto the truck. He got to know the old blind bear that lived behind those steel bars before the fair was over. He learned from the minstrel how to talk to her, and she'd even do her routine of tricks for them. They were like the tricks she did for the crowd at the fair. But with all the noise, she wasn't always able to balance on her hind legs well. With McKindley and the minstrel quietly baiting her with fish and sweetly talking to her, that blind bear could have stood on a log rolling along the St. Lawrence River.

In his mind Theo knew she could help him get through the carnage he saw and the nightmares that bothered him. If Cynthia would look at his nightmares, he thought, perhaps she would in time, become acquainted with his dreams too.

"What do you want in life?" asked Cynthia.

"Oh, Doc, you know me," said Theo. "World peace, cure diseases, save kittens."

"In that order," she laughed.

"Yes," he said.

"Seriously," said Cynthia. "Can you answer my question seriously?"

"I want for no one to have to see what I had to see, I suppose," said Theo. "I suppose I do want that."

"Okay," said Cynthia.

The carnage he saw in his mind did pale in comparison . . . to what they would eventually see together.

CASE FOUR:

"I'm done with the suspense, man," said Friday. "Do you got to come in here and shut me down like this tonight?"

"Relax," Danzel said calmly. "You know, my appetite got the best of me when I heard some news like this happening. I had to visit your town. And I won't stop . . . until I know things are back underway."

"I don't know what you're getting at," said Friday. "My brother taught me not to tell what's on my mind without a what-do-you-call . . . finder's fee."

"Fine," said Danzel, taking a magazine from the rack across from him. "Going rate for the news here is $5.99."

"Okay," said Friday. "I'll tell you for twice."

"Okay," said Danzel. "But I only want you telling me once though."

Friday took the magazine rack from the shelf and said, "Twice the price of the mag or I don't know how else to put this, my man— You my man, too. Trust me on that. It's a fair deal."

"Alrighty," said Danzel.

"Yes," said Friday.

"You recording?" he asked after noticing the red light on the recorder Danzel placed on the counter was lit up.

"Yeah," said Danzel.

"Is that alright?"

"You need recorder to write report?" asked Friday.

"It's to cover my ass," said Danzel.

"I read it in the papers though," said Friday.

"Well then you read my piece demanding more answers," said Danzel. "It's in the same damn paper, Friday. I know you don't know me, but I know you know more about this than anyone who wrote anything about it already. I'm paying whatever price you ask for as long as it's higher than what you told my shallow, puddle-swimming colleagues. I'll pay anything reasonable. Now, forget what you told everyone else. They're chucking spears, but what I want to know is: What's out in the deep ocean?" He paused to let his words sink in. "What do you know about the Sylvan Trappers—Those woodsy maniacs didn't drive themselves out of our town, did they?"

Friday shook his head and looked like he was about to launch into something prolific until a customer placed a few items on the counter for purchase. Friday said, "I'm trying to run a business."

"Do you want me to show the photos?" Danzel removed a large envelope from his folding case. He flashed the first picture to Friday, and he and the customer saw the red '57 two-door Chevrolet convertible. "Does this belong to anybody familiar?" asked Danzel. He flashed another picture of a hand with a wedding band and a few fingers abruptly cut short. "What about this?"

DETECTIVE THEO & DOCTOR VALENTICO
IN
THE CASE OF THE SYLVAN TRAPPERS

THE WIND HOWLED ACROSS THE MEADOWS SURROUNDING THE PLACE. The plate and VIN number were the only clues that lead the way. In the background of the video that Cynthia showed to Theo, there was the old red Chevy two-door convertible parked in a bush, just like it would appear in the photograph later carried by Danzel. It wasn't holding a tag or registered plate, but it had a hot red paint job. "I bet that could have been picked up on a satellite," thought Theo. He found the exact color of the convertible to be *matador red*, and even when the Chevy Bel Air was covered with weeds the matador red held its luster. He matched it to a database who's compilation of satellite imaging included pairing perpetrators that were spotted wearing distinctly colored garments, and those driving distinctly colored vehicles.

Although software like this still showed occasional errors, it provided valuable insight, some tips that Valentico sent to Theodore while he was in the field. The resulting lead was on a dealer that once sold the vehicle in question, so Theo went to talk to the dealer based on that find.

That lead Theo to a car dealer who didn't care to speak about the sale. "You're not from this county," said the dealer. He wouldn't even agree to meet with Bryant. Theodore Bryant started driving through town, looking for a motel where he could sleep for the night, but each one was full. He was feeling out of shape after the short temper he got from the dealer. One hotel manager gave him some hope. He was an older gentleman with greying brown hair and a thin mustache, who said, "Too many people coming through from out of town."

The kind hotel manager had prompted Theo to wonder if any disappearances correlate to the places where the Chevy was seen, which he reported to Valentico. "That sounds like you're fishing," said Cynthia. He told her how exhausted he was before getting over to a possible vacancy. There was news of an inn across town where it would be less likely for people coming in town for conventions to matriculate and fill up all the rooms.

He traveled the forty miles, passing tombstone-filled graveyards where he noticed only the first few rows were convenient to visit; the rest of the graves were covered with weeds.

He stopped for gas when his tank was nearing empty. He went in to pay at the station and noticed a missing person flyer on the glass door for a couple of skiers. Theo thought to ask the attendant about the flyer to see if there were any correlations. He talked about the likelihood at length enough that he could have written an article for *The Crusader*. "The correlations could indicate a perp holding up. It could mean he's got a family captive. Depending what years correlate, he could have . . . started a family by now."

But the attendant didn't seem to be the talkative type, and Theodore was tired and tired of dealing with rude people that day. He paid and went back to his car. But he saw something there, next to the garage of the pump station, that would wake him without needing to find an inn where a room was open.

Beyond the gas station lot was a junk yard with that matador red convertible and a little farther down . . . was a trail he would find that would cause Theo to leave town . . . in a hurry.

The customer got outraged and left the store, causing Friday to lose what little patience he had for the reporter, Jackie Danzel from Louisville, Kentucky. Friday finished counting for the night and slammed his register shut. With a raised voice he said, "You think you can intimidate me?"

"I have friends working in immigration services who would sniff wherever I point their noses," said Danzel.

"So?" asked Friday. "My business has been legitimate since my father handed it over. Those reigns I hold tight, man!"

"Your business? I don't think they'd start with your business, padre," Danzel said with a smirk and the lines on his forehead became wearier. "They'd start with your son on parole. He'd go home to Haiti."

"Alright," said Friday. "Out back in five minutes."

Friday closed the shop door and flipped the sign over, but he stood there and waited for Danzel to yield to his requests before he moved from the door to a smoking stash he had hidden from plain sight behind the register.

He shut off the lights.

In five minutes he met the reporter on the loading dock behind the store with a freshly packed pipe, which he lit, and he proceeded to pass the pipe to Danzel.

"No thank you," said Danzel.

"In my home, it is impolite to refuse offering, any offering, during business transaction," said Friday. "This is my home."

"Offer me something that doesn't trigger asthma then," said Danzel. But he eventually accepted and indulged in the inhalation of burning plant materials.

The monster left his family's farm because he was tired of the bloodshed. He learned a recipe for a drink that tricks the senses into believing the liquid is of human origin. It was certainly nutritious, but he had to put it to a test to see if it actually tasted the same as the juices from the body. Luckily for the young monster, beet juice coagulates like the blood the heart produces.

He didn't stir it so much as he moved the liquid to give it life. He watched it dance in the sun. Large, oily pigmentation lingered, and a thick, translucent film started to build mid-way down the neck of the test-tube size glass. He moved it from the light coming in through the window to the shade at the sill's edge. The monster took the quart of beet juice and placed it on the lowest shelf he could find in the clean stainless steel refrigerator. The light from within the refrigerator and buzzing sounds of machine parts seemed to change the monster. His pupils dilated. He felt a growing rumble in his stomach, so he went outside to sit near the river and pray to an entity unknown to members of the human race. When he finished his compulsive prayer session, he fiddled with wires on a radio receiver that he found on his work bench.

He connected the blue wire to another blue wire and so forth before speaking at a distance into the microphone, "Hello?"

A moment later he got an answer! So he responded, "Hi there. I am calling for our three o'clock appointment." A voice asked, "Can you please hold?" He said, "Yes. Fine."

Cynthia pressed the hold button on her end, and she moved towards Theo's ear to whisper, "Making him hold is a tactic I use with everyone I speak to . . . including you."

"You've seen the tapes?" asked Danzel.

"It depends," said Friday. "What's your angle with the story?"

"Full disclosure," said Danzel. "People deserve the truth. They need me to deliver heroic deeds and write about whatever monsters that might exist. It's the way the world finds out who to trust and who to fear. That's the News!"

"Okay," said Friday, "but what's the price you pay for a copy of those tapes?"

"I'll let you name it," said Danzel. "I've already paid the ultimate price if you ask me."

He poured a cup, ladle by ladle. He took a drink from the tea cup. Something bobbed around in the liquid. It was a thick-red broth, looked like borscht soup when it was warm. The chunks of sponge-like substance revealed tiny hairs, no longer than the point of a toothpick but wider in diameter; the hairs protruded from the spongy-redness in a formation reminiscent of bristly whiskers on a mouse's cheek.

He licked the chunks after stabbing them with a fork and dangling them in front of the camera lens. "Do you want a bite?" he asked. He then claimed the recipe was made entirely of beet roots. Dr. Valentico wasn't sure what to believe, but she knew it was worth reporting to her lover and colleague.

Getting Theodore's opinion had become part of the routine for the doctor. Whenever suspicions came her way. "Because Theo has a lawful way," she always says. She got him to pursue it when she insisted: "He's a maniac who found my ad, and now I need your help figuring out what is the right thing to do."

"I know, don't tell me," Theo said as he relaxed in his lounge chair. He said, "We'll put this house up for sale when they put me in a hole in the backyard."

"That's no way to think," she said, and she sat on his lap. "You'll have to look at the bigger picture. I'm not asking to leave this behind."

"Then what are you asking?" asked Theo. After pausing to

smell her hair, he added, "You'll find everything. Figure out which town we should live in? Find my next place to do what I do, and I have to jump through another set of hoops . . . ? I'm happy here."
"We will be back. We'll make it like a fun trip. It's an investigation. Surely you've taken me around on your investigations."
"Oh boy. Here we go."
"To this day I have trouble actually knowing in my heart that it was all for show," she said.
"I told you. I had a lover, but when I met you, she was . . ."
"Don't finish that sentence," Cynthia said.
"We tracked them for six months. Those petty thieves," said Theo.

"They weren't ready for that kind of hands-on work," said Friday. "The Sylvan Trappers tracked . . . more than for food. Theo and the doctor were hungry too and cunning. Theo hadn't had a lead that was worth his time since he worked undercover with his ex-wife to pick up on a couple lowlifes stealing credit cards. They followed them all the way out West before turning them over to sheriffs there. It was a lawless land out there in the sense that anyone who stood up for principles was the law." Friday took a long drag before he said, "I suppose there's always some law dangling over a man's head."
Friday stopped smoking the pipe for long enough to hail a cab for them, as Danzel said the following: "I promise not to call immigration if you keep that pipe to yourself."
"Alright," said Friday, and he laughed.
"You have my word," said Danzel.

"They weren't just stealing credit cards," Cynthia said.
"Identities. They would sell to transplant patients," said

Theo in way of remembering. "It was a twisted racket. I remember."

"That was big. It *was*. But this is something . . . something else," said Cynthia.

"They were a different kind of criminal," he said. "They weren't in it for the money."

"But he was gross. God awful," said Cynthia with a scowl. "Just from looking at his mug shot I could smell whiskey on his breath."

"He was gross," said Theo with a grin, "but she was smart. She was the brains."

"Certainly. Most women are . . . ."

"I knew . . . you would," he said and shook her off his lap then, and he said, "I didn't find prints from her anywhere. But the camera saw her. And cameras don't lie."

"No," said Cynthia. "They don't lie. That's why I need you to see something."

"Okay," he said and stood up. "I'll have a look. Let me look at whatever it is, in a new light. Tomorrow, okay?" He held her around the waist.

She nodded, but then she swirled her arms around him and she didn't even have to ask again. Instead she bluffed by saying, "I'm going to take care of it myself."

"What?" he asked and stood there as she let go of him and left the room. But he went after her, holding onto some pain in his back that wouldn't let go of him. He was already allowing stresses to manifest in form of physical tension within his body. His muscles learned the names of every person he saw whose life was cut short. With every new victim that entered Bryant's case books his muscles would shout, "We have the memory!"

She let him catch up to her in her office and stopped being frantic when she could tell the pain was shooting all the way up through his spine, enough to make his nostrils jump. And he said, after a long sigh and relieving neck-rolls, "I'll take a look now."

"Okay. Good. So you know, I was going to call the police department . . . after I packed my handbag and figured out where to go next."

"Go pack," he said . . . after watching a few frames of the footage she showed him. Without looking up from the place his flinch held him, in a twisted configuration of terror, he restated, "Go pack."

Belief is something that is more contained than most people are willing to admit. To admit it is to look deep within oneself to find out exactly how thoughts are organized. It is scientific in its own nature. Predictable even. However, belief can also be fluid and it can be a revelation to get to the exact focal point of who we are, what we aim to obtain, and what we are after. Knowing the response to such questions will put someone more in synch with the big picture of the world.

Because . . . . Who are we? What impact do we currently have on this planet and the people that inhabit it? We can change that. We can consciously choose to have a greater or lesser impact with our actions and our voices. When we are pulling back from acting and speaking about our beliefs, are we building towards something new? When we do this, conserving action and voice, eventually the energy escapes on its own, and we often find that we can release the buildup in any direction.

This is exactly what kept happening to Theo throughout the years, even before he met his wife.

Friday tapped on the glass divider to signal for the cab driver to stop the vehicle. Friday said, "Well, here we are—the home of a family that is happily married and expecting a child already."

"You say that like it's rare," said Danzel.

"It's only rare because of wedlock. I'm not traditional—not that type," said Friday. "I can tell," said Danzel. "But it's rare," agreed the cab driver.

The Haitian man lowered his voice to say: "They're still

out there."

"Still?" asked Danzel.

Friday nodded. "Still, man, and here they get married when the cop—ex-cop—Theo got to the end of his leash. He chose marriage over death, certainly. This . . . is as far as I go."

Danzel paid the price and tipped the driver. He stepped onto the hallowed grounds where Dr. Cynthia Valentico and Theodore Bryant made their home. In the driveway was a sedan that bared an eerie resemblance to the convertible from the photograph in Danzel's case.

He rang their door buzzer. They answered. He said, "Hello—I hear tales of not-completely wrapping things up over yonder. According to my source there is much to see."

They showed him the tapes.

"This is sad stuff, doc," said the young monster on the footage they showed to Danzel. "I'm not going to sugar coat it. Just bad. People died to keep my species alive, to keep us fed. Your people died. We're not nice to people."

"What do you mean, 'not nice'?" Dr. Valentico had asked him.

"My people trap and eat you. We watch you, and when you get too close to our hive, we eat you," the young monster said without restraint.

"Where are you located? Your profile says Northeast, U.S.," said Dr. Valentico. She further inquired, "Where exactly are you located, Hewlin?"

"I won't be able to give you that information for my own safety," said the young monster. "I can only give you this meeting and thank my lucky side you are here to talk to me . . . on the internet."

"Mom, I don't think we're right," said the young monster to his mother.

"I know," his mother responded, "and I don't either."

"What?" asked the young monster.

"I'm glad you realize this, son," said his mother.

"And dad . . . ?" asked the young monster.

"He can't ever know," said the monster mother. "He doesn't.... I mean, I don't know if he does do the things... the killings that people in our world do."

"I'm going to follow him, mother," said the young monster, "to see what he does."

"If he is the devil, then you must promise to run like hell when you find out who he is," said the monster mother. "Run like hell boiled over and your feet are made of paper. When life burns you bad, my son, you run away. Do you hear me?"

"I've seen what he does, but that was years ago," said the young monster. "Perhaps he has the change we've had. Maybe ... he hears the warning from within. Does he ... ?"

The young monster peered out the window to watch his father leave the family home. He passed the gas lantern with his blood pole in hand, and he extinguished it since daylight was close by.

The sun would rise in less than forty-five minutes, enough time for the adult monster to make it to the city border, the breeding grounds where the monsters hunt. The young monster knew the way.

He would beat his father there in order to find a vantage point to watch the master hunter at work. "I thought I heard," said the boy's father when the young monster snapped a branch on his trail. "You there!"

His son popped up from behind a pile of logs that had been assembled properly along the state road. He climbed over the logs and found his father's most recent trapping location.

"You ready to help me today?" asked the father of the young monster.

"What happens if I fall in when you're not around?" the monster asked his father. His father's torso twisted in contemplation, much like the oak trees that surrounded them. But his sharp teeth and matted hair scared the child away from his father's gaze.

"You'll fall to your death," his father said. Blunt were his ways of instilling fear in the young monster's heart.

He tightened the harness around the young monster's waist. "One more notch tighter is satisfactory," thought the father.

HEWLIN gave the supporting rope a tug. It seemed like it would hold up, the adult monster thought to himself.

The adult monster gazed through the trees lining the horizon. He thought about a foolish friend that fell into his own trap, not too far removed. That friend was out creating a very similar trapping mechanism on the day that he fell to his own agonizing death. The friend fell down a hole in the ground that was used for trapping purposes, used for trapping prey with wooden stakes and metal spikes that pierced his friend's flesh and ripped through his organs. They could smell the stench of his bowels from the trail, and the monsters had hurried to keep the stench from attracting unwanted attention.

That pit where his friend died had since been deactivated, thought the adult monster. "It was just as likely that pit was cleared of spikes & poison to reuse after burying Tuucinua in the pit that fooled him," thought the adult monster. They continue to make the location an active trap to be known throughout their tribes. There are very few tribes of the monsters stranded on Earth; still, they are relentless to feed to stay that way.

The adult monster lifted the small branches that assembled the outer covering for the trap. While the young monster was taking the branches aside, his father brushed the ground cover of last fall's brittle leaves away. He used the sharp angle of his bare foot to clear the trap's cover. The only covering that remained was made of a lightweight timber, well-known in its ability to crack easily when pressed upon with but little weight.

The trap's interior was a primitive design also: hollowed out bamboo poles, and sharp metal spikes that came stolen from a junkyard in the nearby town of Pheasant Ridge. The group of monsters that survived in the forest land near Pheasant Ridge were envious of the machines mankind would create. So envious were they that they even stole some jagged pieces for their own trapping purposes.

"Take your time. I'll be here if you need me," the adult monster said to his son.

The young monster's red bulb-shaped head glistened in the noontime sun as he used his strength to pull at the rope attached to him. The rope yanked at his harness. He was lifting himself like he practiced. He gently hoisted himself high enough to bump heads with his father.

"If you can lift yourself, you can get yourself back out again," his father admonished. His son was dangling in circles around the plumb-center under the notch marked on the thick branch of a nearby oak tree. He swayed back and forth above the trap's opening. "It's eight feet in diameter at the surface," the young monster thought. He lowered himself, his shoulders brushing against the red clay walls, his ears hearing the echoed crackles of the crumbling clay in the deep darkness below his feet.

The young monster took a deep breath, he looked up, and he saw his father's face. Though the adult monster's face did not soothe him— it bared familiar resemblance, and he gave an encouraging look. For the first time the young monster felt pity for his father. He realized his father had done these trappings all his life. He was old enough to have the internal conflict arise, and he did not know what to do. He pushed the confliction aside and held tightly to the pride that he would one day rise to trap in the way he was taught to trap and eat the corpses that fall to their trappings.

The young monster lowered himself gradually...
    He was three feet below the surface.
        Then, four feet . . . .
        Five.
    At six feet he could see the shimmer of light bouncing off the net from the trap, like a spider's web waiting for a fly. He thought about it like that only long enough to feel some shame in being the spider.

He disengaged the trigger for the net, so he wouldn't get caught and tangled and pulled down to the spikes. With the sandbags locked in place, the young monster untied their ropes from the net for safety. He did not want to be brought to the spikes. "All it takes it one pull of the slippery sheet bend to free the sandbags," he thought. He untied the rope without trouble.

A foot below the net, he found some barbed-tips of metal rods. He pushed one with his foot. It moved with such light pressure to make him shout: "They're loose!"

"Don't worry about it. They'll hold up fine," his father said, holding the slack of the rope from where he stood, on the firm ground above.

The boy pushed his rough hands into his pocket to remove the poison-frog. It was still fresh from that morning walk he took to beat his father to the trapping site. He pressed it onto the steel tip of the middle rod. He mashed its organs along the entire sharp-edged spike. And he left the body hanging there.

"Where the—Hey! Where'd that come from?" shouted his father.

The young monster pulled on the rope. It shifted along the branch above, causing him to jolt close to the poison-frogged rod. His father was quick to pull the rope, absorbing any slack this shift created. Together they pulled. His father continued to brace himself away from the hole. The ascent was not hard to accomplish in this way. In hardly any time at all, the monster breached the surface of the hole. Of course, he reached the firm ground only after resetting the sand bags on his way out. "The net is in place. Nothing could survive that fall," he said to the adult monster. He pulled the rope from the tree branch.

"Good work my son," the adult monster said, "but you have more to learn . . . about . . . our ways of life." They replaced the coverings above the pit. "There's something I should tell you," said his father. He sniffled one time, and the young monster was becoming uncomfortable. When his father spoke with his matted fur and deranged stare, the boy could only hear the screaming of what victims he imagined. He imagined their echoes getting trapped below the leaves and the sticks that must have broken before they were pierced and poisoned. "They are doomed to die," said the young monster before he took to mounting the pile of wood and ran off throughout the forest across the state highway.

His father yelled after him but it was of no use. He yelled, "We were-n't always this way, son!"

Seeing is believing. When she first let Theo look at the tapes, there was no way for him to turn back and hide his impressions.

He sat and silently watched:

A pale haired creature, not man, nor woman, but some other being altogether. It was the same size as a person and shared a similar trait or two with a teenage boy. But it was covered in pale-grey hair and had a snout no longer that a human nose. And its eyes were dark around the edges with a hint of yellow shimmer at center, though I dare not call the center a pupil, for the creature did not appear to have perfect vision. But it spoke English as good as any child in typical social groups. "How about you, doctor?" asked the creature on the video feed while it let out a long, droning sigh. "Have you ever felt like ending your life?"

She had trouble reverting back to her training at first, but she still ended up having a neutral statement: "We have very different lives . . . you and I."

"If you have thought about ending your life, would you tell me? I mean, do you feel comfortable telling me?" asked the young monster.

"I suppose I would," said Dr. Valentico, feeling an incredibly bizarre urge . . . to ask about the boy's appearance. She said, "I've never met anyone like you."

"Thank you for being honest," said the creature. "I've seen people seeing me for the first time and they look awful pale seeing a boy like me . . . looking down on them—In our traps. They're usually dying and looking up to me while I watch them turn pale and . . . ." the young monster paused briefly. "It's a nightmare I have, doctor. That I'm old as my dad. And if I can't rescue them without the others knowing, then I watch their life forces vanish . . . those who fell for our traps."

"Why won't you tell me where you are, Hewlin?" asked the doctor.

"Because," said the boy, "we have been living in the shells of their remains, and we have seen the devil. You shouldn't come here."

At that point in the recording Dr. Valentico had placed the call on mute. On the video recording Theo watched, he could hear her while it was muted for the boy. She couldn't handle it, she wept.

For a publication, after he met with Theo and Valentico, Danzel wrote, "A little convincing was all it took to get Detective Theodore Bryant and Dr. Valentico back on their way to hunting the Sylvan Trappers . . . .

During his visit Danzel had said to them, "The story isn't over. You've got to take to the trail, or I'll take my evidence and finish it myself."

"Blame or bless the nearest person without hassle to who you are, and with a tiny scripture in hand," said a voice on the radio of Cynthia's sedan. She tried to change the channel by moving the dial to the next one, but the same voice was on both channels.

The voice continued, "Have them recite the reason for reason of being alive—" She cut the radio off altogether.

They were in the car driving west, with a few hundred more miles to go before reaching Pheasant Ridge, when the doctor shouted to her husband the following: "Enough already! We're nearly halfway there, and you look exhausted."

They passed a road sign and Cynthia perked up to say, "If you pull off at a motel, I'll pay for us for tonight." Theo looked at the time on the clock of the radio, and then, out the window he noticed a sign for Hotel 66, so naturally, he turned on his blinker to signal to the nonexistent traffic behind them.

They found the place covered in vines, so much so that the sign that stood a few yards away from the building had been caught in the web of vines coming from the hotel. The dark-green leaves had outlines reaching toward the sky, and their veins looked alive and clean. As they walked up to the building, with the sun setting behind them over the tree-lined horizon, they began to question if the hotel was even open.

"I wonder when was the last time these cars moved," Theo said to Valentico, referencing an old dart-in-its-day of a car covered in dust from the Earth, berries from the tree above, and droppings from birds. The tag on the bumper was bent downward and the glass was tinted by time.

DETECTIVE THEO kept watching the same part of the video Cynthia captured. This was his fourth viewing, but Theo gladly pressed play . . . he couldn't find the sleep he thought he would have. On the other hand, Cynthia was fast asleep, recovering from the long drive.

He played the following recording to himself:

"Ain't nothing wrong," the monster in his youth shouted to his mother who was in the room nearby.

On the video, "Every time I look into you—I see how quickly someone is able to switch—to shift from one form to another form. It is a testament to our spirits," said Cynthia. "The brilliant human spirit unifies my kind, and we, too, must be joined, for we are the same . . . save for our differences."

The child slid his hairy fingers past each other, and he said, "It is that which joins us together in our core of being that drives up to great lengths . . . for the betterment of others."

"Those lives ours will never touch with our hands, or speak to with our hearts are still shaped by our actions today," said Dr. Valentico.

Theo turned the video screen off, closed his eyes, and turned in bed to Cynthia. He whispered, "My God. You're perfect . . . in every way."

```
oáobampoonoáheotebáeoehakeeoáto goodoo áoneepoetopeobáeowateroand
oxekotoefxgtnxfxomofeláingoavanxo@atofvanxbunaethxthexteblexoanao

oáobampoonoáheotebáeoehakeeoáto goodoo áoneepoetopeobáeowateroand
oxekotoefxgtnxfxomofeláingoavanxo@atofvanxbunaethxthexteblexoanao

oáobampoonoáheotebáeoehakeeoáto goodoo áoneepoetopeobáeowateroand
oxekotoefxgtnxfxomofeláingoavanxo@atofvanxbunaethxthexteblexoanao

oáobampoonoáheotebáeoehakeeoáto goodoo áoneepoetopeobáeowateroand
oxekotoefxgtnxfxomofeláingoavanxo@atofvanxbunaethxthexteblexoanao
```

"Sometimes things are so frightening in life, we completely shut down to doing what we know . . . is actually the right thing to do," wrote Danzel.

On his own Theo had left the trap when he came upon a bloodied figure that was gnawed to the bone. It looked like raw meat, ripped to shreds.

"We find the need to simply save ourselves," wrote Danzel.

Theo parked outside and beeped his horn, for the lovely Dr. Valentico stood beneath the awning of her home. She moved into the rain, slowly walking toward Theo. They shared their last kiss . . . before getting married.

"We do it for those we love," wrote Danzel. "We save . . . ourselves."

After Danzel spurred them forward, they counted their blessings, for they knew what was at stake for them. Theo rubbed Cynthia's stomach and kissed her pregnant belly. He kissed her wherever he could . . . before they took to the road to find the Trappers Sylvan. They found the whole family.

"You do it because it's right, even when the law says it isn't," wrote Danzel.

Theo had walked from Captain Stegner's office without his support and he wouldn't tell him where he went, or where to find the Sylvan Trappers, so Captain Stegner revoked the department's interest in backing his detective work. Theo turned in his badge and turned to private investigations. He went to live with Cynthia. On their own, Theo & Valentico found the family living in a shack that looked sturdy enough to withstand an earthquake. But . . . it was certainly slanted.

"You tell me he's here?" asked Theo.

"I really think . . . he is," said Cynthia.

"Okay, so we're just going in," said Theo. "We'll take him away and . . . do whatever is necessary."

"And doing the right thing can put you in a bad place sometimes," wrote Danzel.

"Hello—we're here to take your son away," said Theo.

The monster's mother tried shutting the door and said, "No—That's my baby!"

That's when the scraggily haired monster that put those fears in his son's mind started to unravel. He swept the door wide open and said, "Come right in. I have a lot you can get an ear-full of!"

His young son came into the kitchen to hear the monster say the truth. Danzel unveiled it concisely: "This trapper society set the traps with their young and demonstrated demonic behavior . . . only to give the child . . . something to question." The monster said, "You were right to think I was evil, and so were you honey." He embraced his family for the first time ever. "It has been such a tradition in our clan . . . to gain the strong-hold of the family and position ourselves . . . as alphas . . . and to give our children something to question."
The beet juice was ladled out to everyone.

"And what I saw . . . the traps . . . ?" asked the young monster.
"I've silence them," said the monster to his son.
"Are you talking murder?" asked Theo.
Cynthia took Theo's firearm as she passed behind him. Her movements were unnoticed by the adult monster. And Theo swayed around and took his jacket off to further distract as Cynthia obtained an actual stronghold, on the other side of the room.
"M.H. Dog," cried the young monster's father, "but you call me M.H. for short."
Theo took the room with questioning. He raised his tone and spoke viciously. "You got to listen," interrupted M.H. with such sincerity they nearly forgot about the stench kicking up, and there certainly was quite a foul odor among them. Theo cautioned Cynthia to hold her position as he kept talking in a cavalier way to M.H., by saying, "To get a better understanding, I won't drink the red gut blood you're serving up—or your lies."
"I'm serious," said the tall monster to Theo before turning to his son to explain it to him: "I shut them up when I, like you, son, I questioned every evil way. They quit laying traps. It's blackmail." His son moved closer to the door, and Theo comforted him by holding the boy by the shoulders. M. H. kept explaining to them: "What if I'm guilty of blackmail. They said they wouldn't keep it going because . . . I've threatened to go to the police in Pheasant Ridge for years."
"But they're back at it," said Theo to keep the monster's focus trained on him, and away from his wife and her vantage point on the situation. "Here's your chance! You might only get

one." Cynthia sensed a point of no return in the way the conversation had been going, so she cocked the gun aimed on the monster's back. "I didn't realize it would be that loud," she whisper-yelled at Theo.

The monster didn't turn but he did growl. The colors of his teeth and his breath were more startling to the senses than the actual sound coming from his torn vocal chords and winded diaphragm.

"Let's talk blackmail," said Theo in a harsh tone. He cut the room with: "You could have brought it to the police, but you served up lies, and now your people are doing it again. Take the stand. You're all the evidence we need to help you get back to your home planet."

"That was when I decided I may as well drink the cup of red liquid and get an idea of what we were in for," wrote Danzel. "The monsters went away. Their family and everyone drinking the red beet juice was innocent, and it was quite a few trips to take them back to their planet, which wasn't in our galaxy. After the law found out the whole story, it was merely a matter of science.

"It took a few astrophysicists to plot the projected routes that would evade all asteroids and every atom known to mankind, while discovering unlimited elementals along its predetermined route. The projection was more syncopated at determining a new route quicker than anyone who was a bull's-eye at darts, and it was more durable than the finest titanium used to hit a hole-in-one.

"The finest athletes known to our species, and the top scoring contestants on the longest running game show were offered the chance at spinning the wheel of the ship. Technically, the winner of the contest to pilot the ship was no better, or faster than Cheryl Harrowitz, the school teacher who was known throughout the United States for being one of the biggest game show winners—"

All the monsters were found. They weren't offended by the name *monster* either. Actually, they preferred the title *beast*, but they at least liked *monster* because of its notoriety. They were rather chipper beings that spoke lightly and kept their distance. But they certainly enjoyed their own brand of irony.

The ships controls were technically piloted by Quince MacGroy, a profound young athlete trusted by many. Quience had the help of his faithful companion . . . who won the video game contest. The nonchalant co-pilot was the young monster named Hewlin Esquire "Eskalator" Dog.

Young Eskalator wasn't spared corruption of his soul the way his father avoided it, such were the thoughts of his family. It was a fear found out through talking with the young monster's mother and father. In a few sessions, Dr. Valentico was able to get M.H. Dog, the young monster's father, and his mother named Lady Bisbit to sit with her before an organized attempt was made to send the monsters away from Earth.

It was left up the monsters as to how they wanted to control their families—including all types of domestic hierarchy and literally controlling the ships that brought their families away from Earth to their home planet. Cynthia Valentico helped Lady Bisbit and her partner come to a realization that letting their son, Esquire Dog, help out by co-piloting the ship would instill a sense of courage. The reason for reason of being alive helped the young monster overcome any of the corruption his soul felt from being tussled back and forth in his beliefs at such a young age.

Prior to the trip, Danzel wrote, "It was a difficult process sorting the expectations of the monster culture with those of Earth creatures, but they will all be sent from the planet eventually, we think. And the technology was so far safe at launching unguided ships to their home planet. Though linear-light and sound communications are unachievable, the rockets launched so far from Earth have landed. These unoccupied missions to their home planet called Mipsy, have been completed safely in both directions, at least a dozen times, claims a spokesperson for Goose Landings. The main investor of course being the well-known, entrepreneur and bird-man hybrid who wishes to leave Earth behind as well."

History may forget the man, but history always remembers the enterprise. "Ask the Goose about our perishing planet," Danzel thought when he paused writing, "the world gains another Caesar. But more corrupt . . . for he's been plucking out his own feathers."

CASE FIVE:

Theodore Bryant had left the Force and took off to make good for someone that needed his help south of the US-Mexico border. A calling, not the sort that paid but the type that needed help, had Theo behind the wheel and Valentico riding in the passenger seat of her own car. Though, the calling wasn't the immediate concern of either party; rather, they were kicking around some ideas on how to get around undetected. Theo drove the car while thinking to himself, "This woman would have made my previous wife jealous—" before Cynthia noted something without much emotion.

"It's the next exit coming up," said Cynthia, "well, I bet . . . we're halfway through the state now."

She was only letting Theo know that she was paying attention for the last few minutes of their drive through Bezazian County, Illinois. By engaging with him about the subject of tolls, and folding roadmaps too wide for him to be comfortable, she succeeded in buying herself a moment of rest. She nestled her head back comfortably, into the headrest. As a reward for helping the driver feel at ease, she got a wink of sleep. That's deserved for being a caring passenger. And what's more is she helped the driver stay awake.

She said to Theo, an observation that hardly helped at all: "Not many cars. The past hour I have seen two. Both coming our way."

He read her well and said, "I'll wake you when we get to the next town. We'll stop in St. Louis." She nodded and said, "Perfect. Let's become carpet-baggers." He agreed, "Maybe for a day." She said, "Let's . . . rest there."

"Then, we'll load up before venturing through No Man's Land," said Theo.

"The desert . . . is horrible. After St. Louis, I could cry," she said, stirring herself awake. She fiddled gently with her toy, a folded road map.

"We'll be out of the desert and land in a town called Mipskattawhey before you know it," said the reassuring Theodore. "Get your oil ready. I have a feeling we are leaving with a tan."

He wiped sweat from his brow while she adjusted the vents on the dashboard, and he cranked the knob higher to turn the fan up, but they hadn't been lucky enough to have a working air conditioner, so they cracked the windows whenever it got too hot. But they didn't keep them open too long, ever since Theo said, "The dust kicks in more through the window." So they usually settled for filtered air through the vents.

They parked the car in a secure lot just outside of the sprawling Missouri town of St. Louis. A landmark of the expansive enterprise that grew out of the small colonies that built the United States from Portland East to Portland West and then some, St. Louis, was a stroll away from them, across the Eads Bridge. It was St. Louis that demonstrated for the United States what capabilities were in store for the country, during a time when the industrial revolution was at its finest.

They walked in through the first floor of a casino that was anchored on one side of the Mississippi River. The force of water worked hard to move currents downstream and keep St. Louis out of Illinois. The city pulled to Theo and Cynthia from across the river. Big bright lights burned Theo's retinas as they entered the casino, a block off of the Eads Bridge and Bogy Avenue. He stood still for a noticeable amount of time, enough for Dr. Valentico to lead the way to check in; she took him up to a hotel room by tugging on his tired Irish wrists.

In the room she gently unbuttoned his dress shirt before turning around for him to help her with a zipper on her dress. She tugged at the floral-patterned bodice top, with its ruffles resisting her devotion. She started to get frustrated, until she sat on the edge of the bed, near the window that overlooked a main street. Valets working down below their room cleared out all the cars parked in front of the hotel. She kept watching the valets while Theo fell asleep.

The next morning, they rose with quiet anticipation . . . for the day they had planned. "There they are," said Valentico before cracking the top off her plastic water bottle. She drank from it carefully to avoid lipstick smears.

"That . . . hair-piece makes you look like a skank," teased Theo.

"Good . . . . That's the idea, right?" commented Valentico.

"Yep. But I didn't know I'd like it this much. It reminds me of the old days," said Theo. "The disguises we would wear."

"Well, snap out of it. I need you here," ordered Valentico.

DETECTIVE THEO & DOCTOR VALENTICO
IN
GETTING HELP FROM A PIMP AND HIS "REAL GIRL"

WHEN THEY ENTERED *ST. LOUIS*, MISSOURI, THEY CAME ON A MISSION THAT WAS UNDER THE RADAR OF EVERY ENTITY THAT COULD HAVE CARED, BUT THEY KNEW THEY WOULD SOON NEED THE PROPER PAPERWORK TO GRANT THEM FURTHER CLEARANCE. There would be certain parts of their journey where having his detective license in a city in Canada would not be so helpful, thought Theo. And Cynthia agreed that she could certainly see them making use of fake passports and U.S. identification cards if they ran into some seedy individuals.

"Having those types of things, as gross as the people are that we have to go through to get them . . . . I understand," Cynthia said.

They would do anything to protect the ones they loved, and to avoid having anything on this mission traced back to them. Their child at home was all alone with Theo's mother, and she was a strong woman, but they didn't want her to have to deal with anyone showing up at her doorstep.

Theo knew where they would be able to find a new badge and passports, and Cynthia wanted nothing to do with the people they had to associate with, but she agreed the price seemed worth it for the security that they would gain. They crossed the Eads Bridge on foot, in disguise, before they entered a certain establishment where a couple low-life criminals were always holding up.

As they crossed the bridge, they walked from Illinois into Missouri. And from the middle of the Mississippi River, they could already hear noise from this place surpassing blocks of city streets, and the rapid waters of the river. The St. Loose Goose Saloon, where the walls were bursting with vibrations, was pumping and bumping and with music celebration.

As they paused to watch the boats move under the bridge, Theo had some trouble pulling the shiny necklace out of his shirt. He said, "It really hurts my neck, all these fake spiked pieces."

"It's distracting," said Valentico. "Keeps people from looking at your face."

"What's wrong with my face?"

"I don't want anyone to notice who you are—"

"You mean any of my old cronies."

"Exactly," said Cynthia. "I can't share you with them."

"Well, trust me when I say, when Jonesy and his girl know it's me we'll need all the distractions we can get."

"You told the press?" asked Valentico. "I didn't need the press," replied Theo. "Just wait."

As they neared the St. Loose Goose Saloon, they could see the parking lot along the shore of the river, and they had to walk down along the shore to get to the lot. "We were right so far," said Valentico. "They're driving the same ugly moped around this town . . . as the last time you saw them." He looked at his watch and he remembered the last time. He said, "It's a different color, the moped."

She noticed the color of the moped wasn't the boring blue as she recalled seeing in photos Theo had shown. She perked up and said, "That's a news van." Theo said, "Let's go in before they see us."

They moved out from the row of plants on the tile wall garden box before advancing and descending upon their target. They joined the party of Jonesy and his girl.

"They weren't just stealing credit cards."

Jonesy was stretched out, with his arms behind his head when they approached. He saw them and took an overtly relaxed tone when he said, "Good evening. To what do I owe the pleasure of your company? I know . . . I'm violating parole . . . ? That's why you're here, right?"

"Shut up and keep your cool," Theo said.

"Where's your usual girl?" asked Dr. Valentico from beneath dark glasses that she removed.

"My usual?" asked Jonesy. "You got a usual, detective? Or you like to change up who you bring along to see me?"

"This is my wife," said Theo, and he cleared his throat abruptly.

"You want a congratulations?" asked Jonesy.

"No. I want you to treat her with respect."

"Alright," said Jonesy. "I'll try."

"Good," said Cynthia. "Now where's your usual girl?"

A bump under the table shook it good. Jonesy reached out to stop his water and shot of gin from falling over. Out from beneath the table came the gorgeous, long-body of the pale-faced Miss Tricia Kitty. "I was tying my shoelace," she said. "And I got distracted with sucking his—"

"Time out," interrupted Theo. "We're not here to deal-on-about with your personal life. I couldn't give a damn where you put your face."

"We need your help," said the stone-faced Dr. Valentico, while sitting with her hands folded and peering out from over the edge of her sunglasses once again. She looked at Theo, and she said, "He needs a badge."

"I'm not helping you losers," Jonesy said and took his shot of gin. "You can rot and die. I don't care."

"I have a manuscript being sent to my publisher. The guy helping me design the paper I wrote for the Force, called *The Crusader*, he's helping me put together a cover for the tell-all true-crime series. I got a book deal with *Truest-Crime Magazine*," said Theo.

"Once again with the catching up, Bryant. Wifey here. Book tour there," said Jonesy. "You going to tell me you're popping out kids too?" He listens to the silence before laughing. Miss Kitty joins in on the cheerful mood.

"I got you seven years: that manuscript goes out, it's going to be the slammer for you, Jonesy," said Theo. He slid a file across to Jonesy.

Jonesy flipped through the pages of the file and said, "This won't stick."

"It'll stick alright."

"You'll get rid of the whole thing. If I help you, I mean, if— What if I just threaten you. Take you both upstairs. Show this pretty little lady what to do with her bedroom eyes." He looked deeply into Dr. Valentico's bloodshot eyes that still stretched out over the frames of her sunglasses; in those moments, they seemed to stab at him like a dagger would have stabbed. She didn't blink, even when she saw him move towards her pain and vulnerability. Jonesy continued, "Miss Kitty, uh . . . . Tricia. Don't you say the lady has some of the sleepiest eyes you've ever seen?"

"Bed-*ridden* alright," sighed Miss Tricia Kitty. "How about it, lady, you tired?" asked the spotted-fur wearing beauty just before she lunged forward. She was on the table on all-fours with her heels off the ground, giving Jonesy a view of her that was making him fall apart, on his side of the table. He fell so much so that he even said, "You would have to pay for this, detective. Am I right? Well, Kitty's giving you a free show. But what are old friends for . . . ? You Jonesy's good pal . . . ."

Miss Kitty laid the palm of her lace gloves on the chest of Theo, and her left fingers stretched back toward her as she gave him a little push with that hand. Her knees dived down when her hips went high enough for Theo to feel her body weighing onto him. She managed to press hard enough and lift her hips high enough, while folding her knees down gracefully, nearly making contact with Dr. Valentico during the hasty routine.

Cynthia was only mildly startled to find the flexible woman's knees, and spotted tights nearly knocking into her jaw. But before she could react to Tricia Kitty, the seductress had disassembled to a relaxed lean in the booth, next to but leaning away from Jonesy. Tricia looked limber and relaxed, thought Cynthia, so she made a move and took control of the situation, by eliciting a great startle response from within Tricia (and anyone who could overhear the commotion happening at their table). She simply yelled, in a purposeful shrill that was not her usual sounding voice, "Enough! Bold woman! Calm . . . down!"

Miss Tricia Kitty pressed her shoulder blades against the wall she was leaning on and puffed her chest out. She remained internally vivid but she kept quiet.

The patrons at the bar hadn't directed attention toward their booth, since there was a news crew standing outside the St. Loose Goose Saloon that gathered their imaginations. The crew was more of a sight than any sounds from their booth could elicit, inside the typically provocative establishment.

"What makes you think anyone is going to bat an eye over something you write about me, detective?" asked Jonesy. Meanwhile, he lifted his arms to crease and fold his plum-colored sleeves before gently rolling his empty shot glass around on its bottom-end. "Oh, wait. If you were on the right side or the law, you wouldn't need your badge *from me*, and you'd just take me in—"

Theo snapped. He took Jonesy's arm and twisted it. He pulled the man across the table so that his leather vest became pressed against the table cloth, knocking over the shot, and the glass of water he had been protecting up until that point splashed upon the rug. Theo said, "That news camera out there cares. You know why they're here?"

"Let me guess—another base jumper climbed up the Gateway Arch," coughed out the contorted criminal, who managed to sputter words out amidst being tortured.

Theo let Jonesy go, and the freed man made a grand gesture. To which Cynthia responded by tucking her sunglasses far up the bridge of her nose. The news group outside saw there was a scene unfolding, and the anchor with his microphone in hand peered in close through the window to get a look at who was sitting at their table.

With a camera guy and boom operator, the mobile news team rushed to get inside, but Theo was able to beat the heat to the door. He stood in their way, and Jonesy saw how little time he had before they reached him. Tricia told Jonesy, "Get them what they want, or they're putting your face on blast. Those cameras . . . will let everyone know where you are. Do *they* know about Haiti?"

So Jonesy looked to Cynthia for a plan.

Cynthia said, "Okay, here's what I need. I don't care how you get one, but you get us a badge that looks real, but it doesn't need to be real enough to check out with anyone who's legit—we need it to fool someone . . . of your intellect is all."

"Ha," said Jonesy. "What else?"

"We want passports for both of us," said Cynthia, "the whole works on those. We want them to scan and be untraceable. Got that . . . ?"

"Papers are easy," said Jonesy with quick sincerity. "The badge . . . ."

"You're bright enough to figure it out," said Cynthia. "Let's get you out of here." She lead Jonesy to a door that let them out near the kitchen, into the alley-way next to the St. Loose Goose

Saloon.
Jonesy asked, "Is this all going to be in y'all's book?" To which Cynthia replied, "If you're lucky, we'll just draw some cartoons of the two of you."

Tricia was out last, and together, the three of them snuck past the news van on the other side of the building.

"What's the story, Bryant?" asked the news anchor trying to get in the door.

"Deception," said Theo. He handed the news anchor a few bills and the money disappeared. "Just a couple of chumps needed a little bit of a reason to get on the right side of the law."

"It's a pleasure doing business with you," said the news anchor. The guys with him, those broad shouldered crew members holding a camera and boom pole, took their gear to the van. They pulled around the block before taking the decal off the side of the van. The side of the van went from, "Channel 17 NEWS," to ending up as, "Water Damage and Repair? Call Lewis—"

The white building with its red shutters was an honest shop that sold lingerie to all types of people from around the city. It's where the flop-house tramps would go to buy assorted adult items, like clothing and toys they'd use on clients who had high standards for their fantasies. The narrow corridor alongside the beautiful shop lead back to Jonesy's place. That was his private residence that he chose to share with Miss Tricia Kitty, whenever she felt like curling up with him at night. Otherwise, he kept the place pretty quiet.

Jonesy was sweating, hunched over, with a smoldering soldering iron in one hand, and assorted metals spread across the mahogany dining table.

"That had better not leave a mark," said Miss Kitty.

"It doesn't," said Jonesy. He lifted his square sunglasses and squinted at the molten metal. "What do you think?"

"You got their passports?" asked Miss Kitty.

"The papers are being sent out for overnight delivery as we speak," said Jonesy. "I told you that already, doll. It's this damn badge. I can't buy . . . not like paper."

"I don't know if I'm the right person to judge it," said

Miss Kitty. "I've seen too many badges to know which were real or fake."

"You're a lot of help," said Jonesy. She showed him what she's there for, and he loosened up when she snuck a pouch of snuff from his pocket. "You're only after one thing . . . . I'll have to put it through a test of my own," he said.

Out they went to the street to call after a punk teen who was crossing the nearest intersection.

"Come over here," said Jonesy. He flashed his homemade badge and said, "I'm talking to you."

The youth got closer but he stopped in his tracks, a few yards away from the sweaty pimp. The youth said, "Yeah, right! Better go back to the costume store you bought that junk from and ask for a refund, phony!"

"You little brat," said Jonesy, and he reached out to grab the kid. He planned to rough him up for the comment the kid made. But he saw that lingerie shop, and it always gave him ideas to run with. Jonesy let the kid go and he scampered off. Dropping his fist, he said, "Miss Kit, I think I just had one of them mental fixations. You call them, uh . . . ."

"A breakthrough," she replied.

"Uh . . . . yes," said Jonesy. "I would agree."

Jonesy acted fast on his hunch. He called Theo to tell him the good news: "It isn't that easy, you know. I don't exactly have a magical badge fairy factory, and go around *making badge fairies* . . . to make more badges. You don't want one of those rip-offs," Jonesy said.

"Do you have it?" asked Theo.

"I'm about to get it," said Jonesy.

"Do what you have to do," said Theo. "We need it to look the real deal. Just as long as nobody gets hurt."

"I can only promise one thing at a time," said Jonesy. "But I do have to tell you . . . . It's . . . on . . . its way." He hung up the phone.

Almost immediately after their conversation, it had appeared to Theo that someone had already gotten hurt when the following information came through on his police scanner: "Code

Three—reported signs of distress—badly injured—not moving—indicated by rooftop surveillance.... Individual is in leopard print spandex—reports of 'pool of red liquid surround the woman....' "

It appeared that police helicopters had spotted a badly maimed Miss Kitty. Had the pimp went off the deep end?

Theo grabbed his car keys and said to himself, "Don't do anything stupid, Jonesy."

The Metropolitan Police Department for the City of St. Louis, lead by the dapper, bald Colonel Haiden, swarmed the building and started to explore its exterior. One officer went inside after kicking in the door with the thick sole of his combat boot, and he was followed by a few others. One officer went in the bathroom of the first floor, while another officer went up the quarter-landing staircase to the second floor.

"Clear," radioed the first floor officer, who found no signs of distress.

"Second floor," ordered Colonel Haiden.

One officer checked the office on the second floor, while another officer started making his way up the half-landing staircase to the third floor. On his way up the stairs, he tripped a thin wire that had been hidden under the railing of the banister. The wire ran from between the thin wooden baluster and the wall's hand rail. It was dark and dusty, which are perfect conditions to miss the thread-like wire that sprung a trap door built into the landing of the staircase.

The door snapped shut when the officer fell past its opening, and he gravitated down through a dumbwaiter system, a traditional installment left over from when the building was built in the 1950's. The elevator and ropes had been removed by Jonesy, who was waiting with Miss Tricia Kitty. They were in the basement of the building, ready to pounce on the officer that landed on a rather primitively assembled pile of soft mattresses and linens.

"Ahhhhh—" exclaimed the surprised officer on his way down. And he kept screaming as he ripped off his riot mask to gasp for air. "You look just like the woman on the roof," said the officer as Jonesy ripped the wire from his radio. The officer tried calling on it anyway: "I got her in the basement now— That was you on the roof—"

A chop to the officer's neck, placed atop some of his most sensitive meridians, made him go limp. Jonesy picked the pockets of the incapacitated man.

They met outside, a few blocks away from where sirens emptied out their noise. Meanwhile the St. Louis Police searched and found the officer in the basement.

"Thanks for all your help," said Theo.

"No problem-o," said Jonesy, "but you still owe us something for . . . . Well, labor is free, but let's say you owe us for parts . . . ."

"What parts?" asked Theo.

Colonel Haiden reacted fast when he didn't hear back from one of his own. He took to the building on foot, and he was the one to discover the trapped door. However upsetting it was to have an officer attacked and robbed, Haiden reported to the papers, "I'm just relieved the officer involved was pulled from the basement around the same time the paramedics on the roof realized the woman wasn't dead. In fact, she was never living at all. She was made of plastic."

"They weren't just stealing credit cards."

CASE SIX:

Cynthia stops writing and locks her pen away in the desk drawer. She closes her laptop too. She stares at the wall, at a fly that lands above her mantle. And a boy walks by outside her house with a kite. The door opens. It's Theo.
    He says, "If you're still working, I can come back."
    "No, dear!" cries Cynthia. "I'll only be a moment. I'll be out, love."
    When he has shut the door on his departure, she opens the laptop once again, she tosses her hair gently, and she reflects on the screen . . . until she loses focus completely. She tries a counting exercise. "One-one thousand, two-one . . . thousand," she counts aloud. "Three-one . . . thousand."

*

William Lately was fond of few things in life; two of his pleasures were horse racing and fencing. He drank and complained about drinking the rest of his time with expressions like, "Oh, the taste of steel," or, "What a disgusting bit to swallow," and, "Oh! Pucker up and take the pill." He removed plenty of liquid from bottles on the rail at the pub near his home.
    But one day he took the bus from the racing track a few stops too far. Normally, he'd get off the bus feeling like he saved some money by not driving and paying to park, so he would visit the pub he knew so well. When William Lately awoke in another town all he wanted was a bit of the sauce and any taste would do.
    He looked around to find an establishment that would serve him. And he found a place called Anything Goose Pub.
    He had never heard of the Goose or the racket they were running, so he shot off at the bouncer at the door. William Lately said, "I don't want to pay your additional cover." The thug running the racket at the door had no patience for Lately. When Lately asked to speak to the owner, the thug laughed and pushed a buzzer

on the wall.

"Owner isn't here," said the thug, "but there's a lady . . . who will come talk to you."

DETECTIVE THEO & DOCTOR VALENTICO

IN

SHAKEN APART

Part I

"THIRTY-ONE THOUSAN—" counts Cynthia until she is interrupted by the crashing of a kite on the window pane near her desk. She shouts: "Hey . . . you! Don't you know . . . ? Just go play somewhere else."

Cynthia watches the poor child drag his kite away with the string let out at least nine yards. He runs, with it dragging between his legs, until the kite gets stuck in the grass and its string breaks. When she can watch no longer, she turns to let out a huff, an angry sigh. She scornfully slams her notebook onto the painting above her mantel. '*Thwack!*' The fly is crushed, left splattered on the acrylic paint. Flattened and flimsy, some of its body falls to her feet before her heels turn and she moves out to the hallway.

She leaves her sweater hanging on the door knob, as well. The yellow cardigan falls to the floor when she gently leaves the door on its own glide to close behind her.

"I keep thinking . . . about how terrible it was. Lately . . . . Why would he kill himself?" she asks Theo.

He responds after a moment of thought: "Well, there's enough . . . motive. He was lonely . . . for instance."

"Dear, a lot or people are lonely all the while living lives with or without people to share their time with," says Cynthia.

William Lately entered the unfamiliar pub. Dancing girls swarmed each and every corner; most sections of the place the girls outnumbered the customers, who were mostly cops that drank for free. He liked to watch them, but the girls couldn't pull Lately away from the bottles.

Valentico doesn't realize how close she is to the truth that could unearth a crime syndicate that had its hooks in cities all around the world. Yet, her instincts have brought her to dwell upon one of their victims, a man whom she knew personally.

She moves on from this, however... However difficult it may be, she moves on from thinking about Lately any longer, but it won't be the last time her perception receives that sort of shock.

Missis Valentico meets a small group of reporters for statements she's issuing to the press on a slushy January afternoon in a park in the suburbs outside of Montréal. She is reserved, covers her mouth with her scarf and speaks no French.

After introducing herself and making sure they are alone, she dives right in.

"After the first body Theodore found—I shall speak freely and openly now—about my husband's strange manners. You might think he's totally off, but he went through so much in his pursuits and our investigations.

"I will tell my story for the record to show the truth. I am certified to analyze stress disorders. I managed my operations for the public, openly, and as a private consultation more so currently.

"And for many seasons, almost five years, my practice held its residence in an office space not far from my home, in Montréal. It was a charming location to find, despite some construction of the walkway you would see if you visit today.

"My office is in a great neighborhood, and I am grateful for the level of financial security it offers to be in a building with luxury services. At first I shared my space with a massage therapist because I could not afford to rent the entire space, so I shared the third floor with Montréal Centre Du Massage. When I wasn't having a client tell me about their problems, just about every other night, the third floor was filled with the smells of scented candles and lovely lotions that I became well accustomed to, as did my clients. The aroma, it set most of us at ease.

"My neighbors are the International Council of Design, and a tailor called Cutters runs a storefront where businessmen go for overpriced suits to avoid being homogenous in a basic three-piece. A Chinese family ran Cutters up until a year ago when it was bought out. Nobody tailors a suit quite like the Chinese, generally speaking. A few English chaps I've met, like Irving who now lives in Florence, and I suppose the Italians that bought Cutters will tailor a fine suit if you don't mind looking extra *sharp*. This is the type of information I have gathered from male clients who refused to *cut* the small chat and go about talking to me about fashion for entire sessions at considerable length. Yet, still, the bourgeois . . . have problems of their own.

"Although my clients were usually middle or upper class, since they were able to pay a higher than average price for focused attention, I did take a few *pro bono* cases . . . when I could afford. I knew quite a few eating disorders to walk into my office, anorexia nervosa typically. It was not too difficult to treat their fears of gaining weight . . . if caught early on and treated with an aggressive frequency of sessions meant to upset any of the client's misconceptions about diet and nutrition.

"I also treated dozens of persons with post-traumatic stress disorder, or PTSD, which is how I am able to diagnose and hopefully treat Theodore . . . after he *thought* he saw that body laying in that ditch, mangled, and split open . . . like a pincushion. Those Sylvan Trappers . . . spared no expense. They made everything *look* real alright.

"Although my clients have helped tremendously in my understanding this disorder, I have my own experiences to credit as well. And the experiences I have had . . . have nearly stopped me; I am almost unable to see patients in person. I refuse to see new clients in person until I have screened them thoroughly. I no longer downplay the level of security I like to feel comfortable doing my work."

"Soon enough after doing a little marketing in the local phonebook and getting my wardrobe together, things would pick up for my small practice. Considering how most new businesses in my part of town had trouble getting past the first year being open, my practice did fine enough to supply operating costs and give me a steady income, a payroll that my bankers were impressed by, but was really only enough to cover the steady surplus of new clothing and jewelry, since I needed those fancy items to fit in when I would pass by the shops. I was working in a town that wanted women to wake up polished like a shiny, new coin that would call to someone's eye and demand . . . to be picked up. To be put in their *pocket*. I assumed it would make clients comfortable with spending more for my services if I was the shrink who had pearls as large as my eyeballs. Soon I started wearing diamond studs on my glasses, too.

"But I never knew I was tempting them over the edge until one day when a female patient named Darla Henderson snapped at me. She was a new patient who hadn't tried therapy of any kind. She was from Oklahoma and seemed like a really tame woman from the looks of her, really. But she suffered from nervous fits where she would lash out at people around her, claiming ridiculous things, like telling her coworkers that they weren't doing their jobs correctly and that she was always right when they weren't. She seemed to have an answer for every situation, too."

"Well, Darla, what are your coworkers doing to harm you?" I asked her.

"They need to go back and finish their education," she sputtered. "That's what they need to do."

Our initial session went that way, and I prescribed Darla Henderson to relax, take deep breaths, try relaxation exercises, and so forth. The tame woman would turn into a highly energetic control freak without much notice. Darla Henderson suffered from megalomania, a manic disorder where the patient feels their actions are the most important, vital, and a central part of society. The baker that truly feels that his loaves of bread keep the townspeople happy and moving might have a disproportionate ego. But the baker with megalomania is far worse, for he or she truly feels that nobody else in the world knows how to bake bread and the other bakers are out to steal their recipes.

Except Darla Henderson was no baker. She was in finance, working as a tax attorney and public accountant in Québec, for one of the largest retail stores in the province. She sought out a therapist when her employer could no longer tolerate her ways of writing her own rules for how the tax system worked. Darla Henderson had sold her empirical wisdom to her employer for the last time when they were caught following her advice and found themselves fined heavily for tax evasion. By the time she came in to see me she had no problem dropping her tame demeanor and showing how hardened and jealous she was below the surface.

I can still remember how she became unfettered from timidity when she said to me, "You've never had to worry about money, that I can tell. You've been well off, but you're not jaded. Still . . . . Still, you're pampered." She told me that during our first intake session, back when I used to do new client intake sessions in person, like most doctors.

Nowadays, I do intake sessions with new clients over a video chat or phone conversations until I know the client well. And most of the time they pay me for the intake, get sorted out on their own from our time, and send me a cancelation request before we ever actually meet in person. I figured out I have a five percent turnover, including the rare patients I don't want to see again for my own personal safety reasons. I would estimate that of the ninety-five percent of patients that cancel seeing me for their therapy before we have an in-person session, around ninety-nine out of one-hundred get sorted out well enough with our calls and round-the-clock messaging services.

Given that it costs nearly three times as much to see me in person for therapy, I feel that I get to help more people this way, and it offers some safety barrier between me and a threatening individual like Darla Henderson, who nearly ripped me apart with her bare hands.

The *intake process* is what I call my procedure for taking new patients (or clients, as the patients like to be called, but for these purposes we will refer to them mostly as patients). After the attack, when one of my patients suffered a catastrophic episode during the intake process . . . . I knew that my initial exercises needed to be adjusted so as to allow for some protection for myself.

I took a radical approach that has been criticized by many of my peers, and the Montréal School of Psychiatry and Therapeutic Medicines wrote a study based on my notes.

(At this time Dr. Cynthia Valentico produces from her large handbag a document enclosed in a standard size manila envelope. The document justifies what she is speaking about and is easy to find through an internet search.)

After the attack, I spent weeks in my home unable to leave, feeling pained with nerves and unhappy with my unsightly appearance. It took time for the pain to go away, and I knew it would bother me most when I could feel the physical pain . . . as a constant reminder. Throbbing of my earlobes. Oh, they were hard to deal with. In time the scars . . . looked hardly noticeable, much like botched piercings do when done by an amateur . . . in college dorm settings. Theo told me that he likes piercings on women, I remember; that was one of the first forward remarks he made to me.

Darla Henderson had severed the cartilage of my left ear; it was reattached through surgery and some careful stitching done by a plastic surgeon who normally works on the burn victims at the Southern Québec Memorial Hospital Burn Victim Unit. Still, to this very day, if I wear my hair high in a bun, the scars behind my ears are clearly visible, so I don't wear it that way often.

It is my personal belief that no person should shy away from seeking professional guidance, which is exactly what I did when I found myself bound to the feelings that tortured me from the incident. My therapist agrees that I could have brought on a condition in my psyche that I might have to deal with for the rest of my life. We discovered that I needed a way to slow down the number of new people I meet. I especially wanted to meet less people thoroughly in an intimate setting, like in the intake procedures I had been doing.

It can be daunting to see someone who believes they have a problem and wants solutions, while you are strangers to each other. But I couldn't do away with the exercises that brought in new patients. Intake procedures, after all, are how doctors get to know their patients. The process is meant to establish a safe place that allows people room to open their mouths and minds without feeling vulnerable. To allow the organic process to unfold on its own . . . I typically don't speak much during this first visit.

Most patients come referred to her, so the entire intake process only takes one full session, never less than an hour; that's the law for a good reason. But in Dr. Valentico's case, extra care is taken with new patients. In the case of a more serious disorder, such as the person who attacked Dr. Valentico and caused her to be so strict with new patient protocol, patients sometimes stay in the intake process for extra time as the doctor observes. It's a procedure that puts the doctor in the same room with a potentially dangerous patient.

In the case of the person who attacked Cynthia, the doctor was attempting to get the woman to open up. It was the longest intake the doctor had ever heard of; they had seen each other for the intake for three months at two sessions per week for a total of twenty-four sessions, where the patient mostly sat there in silence. She would say things like, "I can hardly hear myself think," or, "You really wouldn't understand." These were typical phrases for a new patient to utter in front of a therapist, but this woman did not look well at all, as she continued to push away from the truth.

One day Dr. Cynthia Valentico was seated in her usual spot on a red velvet desk chair that rolled when she desired, and she was taking her notes when the patient came in late. And the doorman, who would usually warn the doctor when a patient came in, didn't ring the elevator buzzer because he was off that day, so naturally Darla took the stairs.

Darla Henderson came in without warning; she crept through the door to Cynthia's office. She held Cynthia down by her shoulders, bared down on her hard enough for Cynthia to not be able to stand, and when Cynthia did rise from the hold— she held onto the doctor's pearl earrings. They stayed in her grasp until the police arrived. Dr. Valentico locked Darla in her office, and she told the police the patient was a danger to society and to herself.

Oddly enough, a gentleman by the name of William Lately came to Cynthia's mind in a flash during the episode described. Lately was one of her earliest patients when she started her storefront practice in Montréal. Perhaps Cynthia felt safe with the two large oak doors bolted and no other way out of the office apart from the windows. Sure, she felt safe from the rage of Darla.

When Darla came in unannounced, at first, the altercation started as an argument:

"That's right," Darla said. "Therapy helps some people, but for others like me, it feels like a weakness. So every night when I leave your . . . care . . . . I do something." She took the penknife from atop Cynthia's desk. Cynthia grabbed her hand, but Darla was strong, and she flung Cynthia away from her to the floor and across the room entirely. "I do something to prove how strong I am, and to show my body and mind that it will heal all by itself. So do you want to see what it looks like to be a little closed off?"

"Darla, we can still help each other," the doctor pleaded. She insisted, "I'm still learning, you see; I'm not perfect either. I go to see someone to help me sort out my problems in life, so it's okay that you're having the feelings you have. You're not alone,

Miss Henderson; I am right here with you."

That's when Darla Henderson showed Dr. Cynthia Valentico just how strong she really was. On the twenty-fourth session, Darla Henderson rolled up her pleated dress to reveal a series of marks on her leg. "Do you have these too, doctor?" Darla asked before she let go of the fabric synched tightly in her grasp, and she took comparatively few steps to reach Cynthia in order to display her strength on the young doctor's ear lobes.

Dr. Cynthia Valentico felt the fear of death for the first time in her tucked-away, upper class life. She crawled to safety as Darla Henderson made a new mark. She put her foot on the chaise lounge. With her knee raised, she rolled the fabric up once more to make a final incision, telling herself it was to show her body and mind how strong they had become.

A few days before Darla came in and traumatized Cynthia, the doctor had met with her patient like usual. But oddly, without hesitation, that is, she talked about her life for once: "Oh," said Darla, "surely you know the Duke is going away this weekend."

"I had not," said Dr. Valentico, and she waited for the patient to add to her initial assumption. Darla didn't add anything to the idea. Cynthia asked, "Is there anything you'd like to tell me about your fiancé?"

"Yes, well, perhaps," said Darla. Filing a nail with an emery board from her handbag would have gained less attention. She said, "I'm going with him, and it's been arranged . . . and so forth. The company I work for has applauded me for taking the time away to be with my lover." She took a moment to clear her throat and puff her blouse before she continuing: "And they've approved me to be away from your helping hands, meaning our sessions are over. I just need you to write a check mark and sign this form stating I've been cured. Thank you, doctor."

She handed the form to Cynthia, and Dr. Valentico said, "Isn't this something? Well, would you be excited by the trip?"

"Yes," said Darla. "I'm so very excited to sit in smoky parlors while he and a table full of drunks, some of the wealthiest people mind you," she said with a raise of her left eyebrow. "People who drink and think . . . they can buy whatever they want with their money."

"What do they try to buy with their money?" asked Dr. Valentico.

"Oh!" exclaimed Darla with rapture before saying: "Lots." She clutched her arms together tightly before adding with the other eyebrow, "But the Duke won't let them . . . gaze upon me any longer."

Cynthia trembles before the reporters. "I can't go on while the birds in the sky aren't at rest," she says. "She probably relieved herself in fear of Darla," snips one insensitive reporter, among the murmuring crowd. When the birds settle she recalls a time, long before the incident with Darla. A grouping of owls covered the Edward VII Monument at Phillips Square.

"I wasn't far from my office when the owls came into my life," Cynthia admits to the reporters, "when I planned to meet a client I wished I could have helped more. The flock of owls only left occasionally to pickup mice or other tasty foods from around the monument of Edward the Peacemaker," she tells the scoop of reporters. The owls were obsessed with talking to Dr. Valentico, and they appeared there in Phillips Square to hoot at her as she walked by each day. "I remember it like Edward himself was speaking to me."

They became intrusive eventually, and the owls might have done better blocking the door to her office on Rue Le Royer Ouest. "It was enough. Thanks Ed!" she shouts as she returns to her normal ways, and the crowd has settled, as well.

The owls began to realize which people went in to visit the doctor, and before long they started making noise whenever the dapper William Lately would pass by the public square, since he was usually in the area to visit for his appointments. Cynthia recalls hearing from the doorman about a time a car pulled up to the building. "It was after Lately had entered for . . . his last session," she says with a long swallow.

A woman with pointy red hair stepped out from a sharp car, after badly injuring one of the owls outside. She hit one of the birds that was focused on Cynthia's office with her car door. The metal door of her Mercury Marquis acted as a meat cleaver to the perched owl. Sybil Deville stepped onto the brick in front of the fountain and entered the two-story office building when the doorman ran outside.

He yelled at her: "You hit one of them. I've been watching them for days." He cowered near the bird with its twitching wings. But Sybil went right in without hesitation. She went up to see Lately without signing in with the doorman, who had abandoned his post at the front desk.

The drunken Lately asked her when she entered the room about her parking job, but Sybil just smiled with her slick hair blocking her left eye in a sharp, angular way, and she said, "You're relentless, you are—"

Watching the doorman move the dead animal while all the other owls flapped around him is something Lately could not resist, and so he stayed by the window to stare out. He said to her, "Babe, you're the relentless one to follow me all the way across Québec. I know you're into me." He hiccupped and said, "But you'll have to wait until after my therapy appointment." He hiccupped once more and said, "I'm sorry . . . about the mess in the waiting room." Lately had vomited in a trash bin on his way into Cynthia's office, but Sybil had no intention of sitting in the waiting room. In fact, she hadn't even been listening to Lately at all . . . because she was busy trying to find a way to tie a rope around the sprinkler system.

"Why do you need to stand over me," said Darla, "and judge me the way you do? Like you're so perfect anyway. Because you went to school to understand the way—the way the mind works. Suddenly you think you know everything about the human condition."

"My job is to help you," said Cynthia.

"You can help me by letting my company know I'm okay," said Darla. She was still calmly sitting on the chaise lounge at that point.

"I can't do that yet," said Cynthia. She adjusted herself in her red velvet chair and swung around to her desk.

"Sign the form," demanded Darla.

"I can't sign it now," said Cynthia plainly.

"If you don't sign it," said Darla, "then I can't go with my fiancé and if he loses the tournament, that's on you!"

Dr. Valentico moved her pen in quick succession to make narrow cursive letters on a page in her notebook. She said, "There will be more tournaments. I'm sure you can explain it to him."

"Sure," said Darla in a low voice. "He's not going to have time to . . . focus on anything I explain to him . . . but sure . . . . I'll tell him why I can't go, doctor."

"It was terror, but it didn't matter. The terror had to stop," says Cynthia to the reporters before she describes the moments after she fled from Darla. When pressing her back to the door, she was able to slide to the ground easily. The entire time she thought of the peacefully disposed William Lately.

It was right from boarding school to prep school, secondary school for girls, to an all female conservatory where Cynthia studied health and human services before getting her master's degree in Human Psychology and Psychotherapy at an Ivy league school. It was all done to land her . . . on her bum. Broke. But hopeful since she was in business. That was when she met Mr. William Lately.

"Darling," said Lately, "you look . . . worse off than I do." They met in a crowded public café before she had the office she would rent. But the wealthy Lately didn't mind the crowd. He was content, since he saw Cynthia had a stirring desire to help him sort out his problems.

Cynthia thought Lately was an easy patient, but she also feared she was at a loss in representing the healing process to the man. For even though he had an easy-going, wonderful disposition as a person, Lately did not want to be healed. She recalls to the reporters, "William Lately lived alone, an aristocratic-type, apparently entering his second leg of life with no real passions. His love-life was ambivalent, and his family removed themselves from him over time. His fortunes from unknown ancestors were dwindling. He did not love himself, so he did not try to heal himself."

D<small>R</small>. CYNTHIA VALENTICO meditates on William Lately and how she thought the usual way doctors conduct their intakes of new patients was a safe way to test the waters—for William it was—He was safe; therefore, so was Cynthia. But the doctor was clearly wrong about Darla, but it wasn't Cynthia's wrongdoing since Darla lied about her history of mental breakdowns and substance abuse.

She'll never be able to forget that incident . . . nor Lately's incident. She wishes she could have helped the man who felt to her like someone she could see herself with one day, and she wished she would have been there more to guide him and help him heal. He needed guidance, and she could have loved him. But she wasn't there in time that day, and if not for what the owls would do, she might have went on thinking he took his life. She admits, "I had been falling . . . . Excuse me. I had been feeling . . . like it was all my fault."

When William Lately entered the room to talk to the doctor for the first intake session Dr. Valentico felt the emotions he had were hard for him to interpret, but they were clear to the doctor. "He seems to be missing a remaining part of the chain that holds people to society," Cynthia reads aloud her notes on Lately. To the cameras, she smiles and admits the faults of a young doctor. She says, "The last shred of dignity Lately holds onto he thinks . . . is only just enough to be tolerable. But he is . . . most impressive. He's a feral man who never forgot how to hold onto his last thread of self dignity. With a kind smile and polite demeanor, Lately never arouses any . . . unwavering feelings." And she went on believing he had no unwavering feelings, that is, until she knew him no more.

She would say to her client, "Good evening, William," if his appointment was in the evening, or "Good morning, William," if his appointment was in the morning, but no matter what time it was when she greeted Lately, he would always reply ever so softly, "It is good." That was Mr. Lately. In few words, he was short.

But as these moments faded away, Cynthia was on the

floor holding bits of her ears, with other parts of the fleshy lobe still in her office within Darla's grasp; Cynthia felt disjointed and broken. The soft, kind tones of her kind, tender patients were not to be found. No more Mr. William Lately. The early memories . . . had all disappeared. She heard the floorboards creak! Behind the door! Then, the door started to tremble against Cynthia. She moved back to brace herself against it—pitted against the floor and spreading her crimson blood along the white paint, she held on strong for a few moments more.

"Darlene," misspoke the doctor, "the police are on their way I'm afraid. I'm afraid you've gone too far for me to help you, deary."

The doctor heard a soft, low groan before Mr. William Lately's finely tailored vest, with its green and gold plaid, came to her mind's eye. His suits had always fit to him well without being the least bit snug. He may have well wasted his fortunes at the tailor, although he was meager enough about purchasing new clothes. He wore the same few suits since he never really changed weight all that often.

There he was, looking sharp as ever, hanging there by the window of her office. She went on thinking he tied the rope himself, around the water pipe made for the sprinkler system. It was just high enough to see down and out the window, to see the pretty little fountain where young, cheerful couple would go for lunch, and where workers would take their breaks. Cynthia liked the view so much, so that she softly imagined to herself that William Lately saw a lovely scene as he died there in her office. It might have been a relief if she had known that William was watching the doorman help the crippled owl.

"I was confounded with horror and frustration, but I didn't let these feelings stop me," she says to the scoop of reporters. "I convinced myself it wasn't a real threat but more of a challenge. Just like how I felt grateful to have been in William Lately's life, and I felt I learned a great deal from being in his presence. After his death, I would eventually feel more ready and prepared to help people like Lately. If I only could have known then," she tells herself, "I would have been able to help fix Lately."

Since his death, she believes she has helped save other people, yet there are many more cases like the dapper gentleman she could not heal. But her despair from being attacked by Darla caused her to recoil greatly. She decided to change her procedures for taking on new patients after Darla Henderson left her storefront office space sealed in a heavy vinyl body bag.

Part II

Later that night, when she was lying in pain, Cynthia found a note in her hospital room that helped lift her spirits some. The information contained on the note would change the course of her life and very existence, forever. It was a step toward having endless adventures with her true love.

The note was next to a pot of primroses:

"You'll be okay, that's the best advice one worker of the minds can deliver to another like yourself. Get some rest and heal up."

Despite her pained situation, Cynthia appreciated the gesture and instantly knew who sent the gift.

The note continued on:

> "The world still needs good doctors. Sorry you had to take one for the team, but your efforts have been noted. Give me a call if you would like to work with our department, and I'll keep an ear out for any open position, Doc. —Theo"

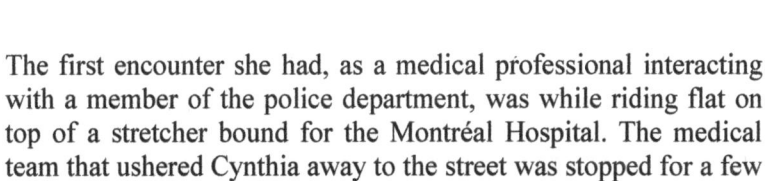

The first encounter she had, as a medical professional interacting with a member of the police department, was while riding flat on top of a stretcher bound for the Montréal Hospital. The medical team that ushered Cynthia away to the street was stopped for a few moments while the police were piecing together the information after finding Darla Henderson's death and suicide.

That was when Theo first came up to Cynthia to introduce himself. She had already laid flat on the stretcher and given into the medical treatments available. By the time Theo approached her she was already wrapped in bandages that resembled earmuffs. They were to stop the bleeding.

He first approached Cynthia wearing blue latex gloves, but

he took them off, rolled them up, and tucked them away inside his pocket. His hands were smooth and warm when he reached out for her stretcher and patted her on the bare shoulder.

"It will be okay, Doc," said Theo. "How well did you know the deceased?"

She wasn't responding, so Theo referred to a small handbook of French phrases, but before he started speaking the language, he tried asking her, "Madame, can you hear me?"

"I'm thinking," she said. "I don't have my notes. Forty-seven days, I believe."

"Sorry," said Theo. "I thought maybe you didn't speak English—" He quickly changed the subject with: "You are going to be alright. It may not seem like it now, but this kind of stuff happens . . . the longer you stay working in your field. You're bound to come in contact with some really strange characters. Just lucky you got out . . . alive and unharmed. I'm assuming those are piercings you have . . . ?" Cynthia smiled a tiny bit. Theo continued, "I love a woman with her ears pierced. Bravery makes fond partners with beauty. You're going to be alright."

She let out a sigh and said, "I will, but I won't be able to see patients, not like this . . . not anymore. And Darla . . . . What a shame." She let a stream of tears flow as the medical team carted her away to the ambulance.

She tells the reporters, "That was when I started thinking about how easily it would be for another patient to do this or do something even worse to me during a session." She told the scoop how she started thinking about changing her process altogether.

In the hospital, her main concern was no longer survival but a fear of the tremendous cost of medical bills, for health insurance covered the cost of her dilemma only partially. Some of those expenses would need to be taken care of through careful litigations with the estate of the deceased. And luckily for Valentico, Darla had quite a sizeable sum of money behind her name. The deceased was engaged to be married to one of the most profitable gamblers in Montréal, a man formally called the Duke of Framingham. He earned his name only after winning enough that he could afford to pay the announcers at every poker tournament to call him what he preferred to be called.

But Cynthia quit occupying herself so drastically with the possibility of an emotional dispute over money. Since the doctors at the hospital were able to put her ears back together, the only immediate concern for Cynthia was the property damage she was responsible for since she had a guest that caused the damages, and she felt saddened for the loss of life, of course.

"I'll need money to cover the situation with the property damages," she admits to thinking to herself, "to at least start a payment plan with the owners. But even more, before I'm going to feel comfortable working with new patients again . . . I'll need to redefine my practice."

"Oh my Darla," sang the Duke as he entered. He was mocking the tune of "Oh my Darling, Clementine" when he sang: "Oh my Darla, Oh my Darla, you were mine!" He stopped to get close to the doctor's face to say to her, words no medical professional wants to hear: "You didn't do enough of your job, you witch doctor!"

When she came to again, the Duke was gone, and she thought maybe she dreamt that he visited. After all the bleeding had stopped and Valentico was properly stitched up, she stopped at the front desk of the hospital on her way out. That's where she saw the signature of Joseph Cluster from Framingham, Alabama.

The hospital's logbook showed the Duke was the only guest to visit her, which made sense since most of Valentico's family were deceased. Her grandparents retired to live in Florida, and her parents had disowned her when she started using large words and buying finely made accouterments that her father could not justify on a logger's salary. Nobody else was signed in to visit Dr. Valentico, save the courier who brought the flowers, and the sobbing, grief-stricken man who had just finished in third-place at "the All-or-Nothing Black-Jack Tournament" in Copenhagen, Denmark (known as the happiest city on the planet). He was sitting with a big stack of close to $40,000 on a $10,000 buy-in. It was enough chips to lead the pack, but he went on tilt when he heard what happened to his dear fiancé, Darla Henderson. Cluster did not bring happiness back with him from Copenhagen, unless it was sitting in his luggage and waiting to be unpacked when he visited Dr. Valentico.

"I remember the off-kilter way in which his voice disappeared as it seemed to be swallowed up by the hall outside my hospital room." She stops talking long enough to recall the way he sang it: "Oh my Darla, Oh! My Darla, Oh! My Darla, always be mine."

She took the note and went in to start working as a consultant to the police department in Montréal, helping with the overflow of psychiatric evaluations at the precinct nearest to her hometown.

She reminded Captain Stegner of the way Theo was when he was new at the department when she was shocked by how understaffed the medical counselors were. When Theodore first came in, it was during the afternoon. It wasn't typical for the head of a medical assemblage responsible for thirty of their own clients to be a high-ranking official who protected the peace and order of their city, while filing their own paperwork. But Detective Bryant wore the responsibility then with honor, while he served with the Force.

He slacked off when helping on cases when Stegner was the captain overseeing his work, but Stegner didn't give him much grief then because he knew Theo had to stay fit enough to run the Force's Internal Investigations for as long as his nerves could last. Some of the sergeants and even a lieutenant at the Force took bets, on a regular basis, as to whether or not Bryant would crack under pressure. And they speculated on which tumult would be responsible for chinking or cracking his armor.

Actually, there wasn't much of an internal untit when he transferred out of Border Patrol and Customs to join as a full-fledged, uniformed member of the Montréal Police Department, so what Valentico saw of the MPD's Internal was very much devised by Detective Bryant.

When Bryant first moved in to be an investigator for the Montréal Police Department— shortly after the crossing of a young kidnapped girl named Henrietta Blake—Theodore Bryant started out at the MPD as a cadet, but he quickly found his niche in there, at the Force.

He walked in, right up to the desk, and he spoke directly to the face of the sergeant behind the counter. And he said, "Have you seen where guys start out over on your side of this conversation?"

The sergeant assigned front desk duty that afternoon played hard of hearing: "What?" he asked the eager young Bryant.

"How do they go about it?" Theodore smiled a friendly way. He waited a cordial moment before launching into, "Do they go in through that door there after talking to you first?"

"You're damn right they do. I'm Ross McKindley, and I've seen you around." Back before McKindley had been promoted to lieutenant, when he was still the humble-sounding sergeant, he leaned on a stack of magazines and files he had been shuffling together all afternoon. "Are you related to Nancy?"

"That's right," replied Theodore. He said, "I knew you through Cousin Eddie" —a friend of Theo's— "when he married Nance. We met . . . at the soccer game I think."

"That's right," said McKindley. "Why-where are you working these days? Don't tell me you're looking for work. We really don't have room for a cadet, and you don't want a desk job here, kid."

Little did Sergeant McKindley know, for Detective Bryant would take on the role of cadet in training. But it was with a caveat that he be promoted to sergeant as soon as he could cover the department's stingy need for Internal Investigations leaders. At that time, Bryant was the best leader Internal could hope for since he had been trained to read psychiatric symptoms and other signals as part of his duties when working with Border Patrol and Customs, and the mentorship requirements he performed during his graduate studies with a notable published medical professional spurred him into police level undercover work prior to applying with the Force. Cadet Theodore Bryant would make sergeant as soon as he helped the MPD organize their Internal Investigations. It was something the department desperately needed but didn't have the budget to hire.

It was a hard job running Internal Investigations, and Dr. Valentico understood how much pressure Theo was under when she saw the stack of files in Bryant's office. Most of the files were duplicates for Bryant to review, but a stack on top of his double-decker wooden file cabinet was dedicated to his own detective work with the Force. Sergeant Bryant answered directly to Stegner, while as a member of Internal he answered to nobody.

For Dr. Cynthia Valentico, when she first became a consultant for Internal, it was a part-time gig for her to take on three to four intakes a week who were under review for their badges at the department in Montréal. There were a few others, like Valentico, that were hired on as consultants to review possible future cadets. But Valentico was given special permission by Theo to review applicants however she wished, so she set something up that she could replicate for taking new patients in her practice as well.

"However, I had great certainty I wouldn't see those patients again," Valentico tells the reporters in the park after one reporter questions her role with the police department.

"Dr. Valentico, can you please tell the press about your role before assisting on the case outside of the umbrella of Internal Investigations?"

"My job was to weed out the nut-jobs. Everyone else I would send as referrals to Internal Investigations, at their desk on the main floor of the MPD office, or I would inform the precinct where the applicant was visiting."

When Cynthia Valentico joined as a third-party consultant she kept running her practice in the same shared office space she had when Darla Henderson attacked her. The space had been renovated after the incident: the new skylight was a popular addition to her office. She welcomed something new, so she stopped taking new clients in her practice while she came up with a distinct, new intake process— one that would guard her from the types of people she had grown to fear.

"I saw over two-hundred applicants that made cadet the

first year and weeded out another six-hundred or so who weren't fit pipers. That was over the course of a year and a half if you count the time it took to come up with my system for intakes," she tells the reporter. The papers would publish anything they could get on the record from her or anyone involved with the Sylvan Trappers, the ballooning family, or any of the other high profile cases she would eventually work on in her career.

She tells the reporters, "It was when I met the Captain [Stegner] that I became engaged in a discourse on what it means to be undercover. It is something I wanted never to use, but it certainly came in handy later when I was forced to decide between assisting in the hunt for the Sylvan Trappers or living tucked away from justice, and I knew the time would come to open the gates again. It was at the fair with Theo that I learned the value of pretending to be someone else. It's a skill that helped me stay alive later on."

Like most women, Cynthia enjoyed talking to Stegner, for he was knowledgeable and always a polite, professional chap. It interested Valentico that he was writing novels for the true-crime genre. His nonfiction-style tales outraged many working professionals, even beyond the MPD. For, in those tales that made Bonnie and Clyde seem like second-rate novelty, nothing was off-limits. And that meant that no badge was safe from showing up in his writings either. He learned the ways of implementing great creative prowess, a daunting task to many people.

But Stegner's written and self-published with some success. Here's an excerpt from *The Review* that even goes as far as to give him credit for inspiring Bryant: "It was the writings of Captain Larry Stegner that inspired Theodore Bryant when he left working with the Force on cases as an active agent and concentrated on writing news reports to inform some of the members of the Force. The police learned to rely on the information Bryant gathered in his reports and would pay for them even. He came in with experience enough. He left the Force only two years into his service to pursue his own publishing. But he always respected where he had been and who he had worked with."

The Case of the Sylvan Trappers called Bryant out of his

jurisdiction, and he went through with the investigation despite his withdrawal by the captain. Even without a badge on his belt, Cynthia explains, "He knew that Captain Stegner would sympathize if anything went wrong, at least he hoped so."

The captain had broad shoulders and always dressed in a suit without a jacket. And he wore suspenders. He liked to enter conversations, talking about stories he was working on. "You never really knew whether to take what he said as the truth, or as fiction," says Cynthia. "Either way he was a great storyteller." He never got insulted when his subordinates would interrupt in confused statements. "What?" or, "Start over." Or "Slow down," was another common reaction when Stegner spoke to his crew.

"New moves made to lower arms within the CIA bringing our boys closer to heroism and one guy closer to finding his heroine—"

"What are you talking about, Captain?"

Stegner handed over a copy of his latest novel to Ross McKindley, whose job it was to spread the news to those that didn't already have a copy—most of the members of the department were too busy or too tired after filing paperwork on their own to read the fine investigative reporting.

Dr. Cynthia Valentico once stole away a copy when McKindley wasn't paying attention, and she carefully hid away from plane sight . . . to read over Stegner's reports.

"What the destructive tendencies must do to their hearts . . . . 'I fear the damage to some of the members of the department would be irreparable. It was that way with everyone,' Stegner wrote a storm of notes on the department. 'The ghosts those men and women must have saw, they haunted their darkest nights,' " she tells the reporters. Cynthia believes she saw the shadowy nature of the cases and the ghostly remnants, but did she really see them . . . ? All the stories she heard from members of the Force, talking about people being kidnapped, and taken to be tortured, or sold, or killed; those stories stayed with the person telling them, and they told their stories to the doctor . . . in confidence that she would not utter their words. That she would not repeat their stories, their personal experiences. But she must live all her life knowing they happened, and there's nothing anybody can do to help them. But some of their ghosts won't stop calling to her . . . from the shadows beneath the darkness.

Those departed souls that haven't and won't quit must have known the witnesses to their cries would talk to someone if they only rattled around enough. Some of her patients were rattling on and on, for they thought they had found the doctor to help them while being in the worst possible conditions. These were the people torn between suicide or insanity. Perhaps it was Lately who helped ready Cynthia, for when she started working with Internal Investigations . . . she felt like she was ready to help others find a way.

Working with new applicants to the department meant her job was structured to keep her identity secure by using video and audio interviews to process each new applicant. For all instances, Dr. Valentico structured her agreement with the department so that she never had to commit to a case, or patient rather. Incidentally, she would abstain from referencing her work by case at all. Her agreement with the department was to take on *discussions* instead, and they never had a resolution attached as a requirement. With all other cases that she assisted in with the MPD, she would insert herself into the clinical healing process at whichever point herself and Detective Bryant agreed upon. They needn't really consult with the patient, since their jobs were mandated as a requirement through Internal Investigations. In fact, usually patients were pushed to speak with a doctor without a choice in the matter. Technically, the only choice for the individual would have been the alternative, a retirement from the police department.

All cases were sensitive and required Bryant and Valentico agreeing on the timing of Dr. Valentico's "addition to the discussion" as it was laid out in her contract with the police department. Her choice of cases with "recommendations considered" meant if Bryant wanted her to help, it was always up to her to fulfill any requests. In other words, she had a hard angle on the foot they let her have in the door. Bryant felt that was the way it had to be after the attacks she had endured at the hands of one of her patients.

"Detective Bryant was seated behind a table at a booth at the fairgrounds when I first saw him outside of the office, I mean, the department. It was the first time I agreed to go on an undercover sting and the first time Bryant was leading such an operation. It was a relief to see his task-force was up to their knees in volunteers, which meant my job was done right. Seeing as the festival staff worked with Bryant's undercover police squadron *through my assistance*. I made everyone on the squad look more legitimate and less obvious," says Cynthia. She pauses to collect herself being continuing:

"But, to be honest, since I'm going over the emotions again, I should add, that to be fair, I was shocked that Theo could act like he didn't even recognize me outside of the muted white walls of Internal. He was more concerned with finding the target, a Spanish Ambassador who was part of a smuggling ring built to compile arms codes. Their network of traders helped distribute arms codes to the CIA's Most Wanted List. And it was the job of the undercover squad to keep the most wanted criminals starving for weapons, because their unarmed platoons meant less skirmishes and loss of valuables. Too many lives were already dreadfully lost; to top it off, most of the members of the squad were sergeants or lieutenants who had already been personally impacted by members on the Most Wanted List, so they had a great incentive," says Cynthia before taking a question from the reporter from *The Review*.

"Jackie Danzel, *The Review*."

Everyone laughs and the reporter looks confused by their laughter, so Cynthia clears up the tension by saying, "Most of us know who you are." The dozens of reporters and spectators present settle down their laughter before Danzel continues speaking:

"Well, they're who's paying the most for me to be here today. Hoping to get a good story together that shows you and your husband at odds, but I haven't found one yet," says Danzel.

"You're looking for a story of us feuding," says Cynthia

with astonishment on her breath.

"Crime doesn't always pay well," says Danzel. "This week they want to hear about getting through tough times, the motivational type, not too romantic, or down-beat, please."

"Well, I don't know what to tell you, Danzel," says Cynthia, perplexed.

"Yes, well," Danzel twitches his pen on pad, and he starts saying, "You skipped over the part where you ruined Bryant's operation. What exactly did you do when you saw Theodore on stage as a magician at the fair?"

She grows bright red and laughs, somewhat nervously, and she says, "You should hear Theo's side of the story. He was afraid I blew the whole operation." She searches for a blurry-looking picture of the man she describes. It's hiding among her files. She shows the entire scoop, but Danzel clings onto the picture the longest. He takes it with him and leaves the conference altogether, after getting the details he needs for his story.

"The contact had so far only revealed themselves as his title dictated, 'The Ambassador.' He let the department know he'd be wearing business attire, and they were really placing a considerable amount of faith in his proclamations. He told the MPD, through letter: 'My services to the world are my leverage but I will remain unnamed to you.'

"It was a lot of responsibility for Theodore Bryant to take on, for when he worked for the Border Patrol, that was one of the first real positions of authority he had held. Before BP&C, he never even had as much authority as a crossing guard. Even in grade school, his teacher passed him up for becoming a hall monitor. Having people look at him with respect was something Bryant relished in at the beginning of his role leading the squadron undercover. Of course the feeling got to him. One day he had this false realization when I asked him, during an early meeting as friends, mind you—we weren't dating yet, and he wasn't sitting in a therapy session— I asked him what he thought the world thought of him, and he . . . thought there wasn't much to think. But he saw his place in the world and it was fighting for something he believed in upholding: the type of regulations he enforced during his time as a Border Patrol Officer were matters of public safety."

During his time at BP&C, Theo turned a blind-eye to matters that he understood to be benevolent bureaucratic nonsense. He found rifles unregistered but with a sincere hunter. He found small caches of hard drugs, and a few large shipments of marijuana (including a guitar weighing over forty pounds without its case). If it looked like a situation that needed intervention, he would certainly have gotten himself involved. He found a parent once, for example, mistreating her children. She had an open container of alcohol; he got her locked up for that to separate her from her children long enough to help them get the help they needed.

It was his job during his service as a Border Patrol Officer that helped him first notice the importance of finding missing children. In fact, there was a certain child that left his post one night with a man who was posing to be her father, and that child was Henrietta Blake. But the imposter . . . said her name was Jess-Belle.

When Cynthia finishes with the press conference in the park, she returns to the precinct that houses Internal Investigations. "That coat is a disaster, I mean, our uniforms are issued to us and they don't even look like that. What color is that? Trout? You've got to go shopping for a new one if you're going to fit in around here," says Lieutenant McKindley, who was no longer running the front desk at the department in Montréal.

After such an event, Dr. Valentico doesn't care about fashion or the way her reflection appears, but she does know all the people shuffling past her in the city will turn their noses up and some might even refuse her services if she doesn't look right for them. When she picked that spot to work in the city, she didn't realize these types of challenges would face her frequently, for no middle class person—as she was raised—will go into her office because they fear her services in that part of town will deplete their back accounts, so she is left to help certain people who don't care about how much she charges. She is able to charge a fair price, too, but it's reasonable to the people above the bourgeois, which means she has fewer clients coming in to make the salary she feels she deserves. She can afford to pay for her medical school bills and pay them off early, too, but how unfortunate! She never realized how one incident could cause such turmoil for her.

"Now that you've taken over completely," says Theo. "Of Internal Investigations, I mean."

"I've taken over," Cynthia says with amusement, "more than Internal. I hope." But Theo gets uncomfortable and moves from her to say:

"You're lovely. And I want to give you everything. So I've decided to tell you the truth."

"The truth about what? Theo? What are you telling me?"

"What if I told you I know more about William Lately than you might like to know."

"So tell me."

"I am."

"You are what?"

"Him."

"Hmmm?"

"I am him."

"Hmmm—what?"

"What if I told you that I *am* William Lately."

"What?"

"Well, he is me. He's a character I created to go undercover when we saw the type of clientele who visited you." He looked at one of her scars.

"Couldn't you have told me?" asks Cynthia.

"It was before I knew you, before you came to work with the Force."

"I know but," she says and she notices he's looking at the scar on her left earlobe. "You were watching what type of clientele came in?" She's enraged with the memory. "You mean Darla? The woman who ripped—You were undercover to watch for the Drake Family through Darla. I get it. You used me."

"We kept watching your office, and that shoe box contains all you need to know now that you're running Internal. And I promise you . . . . Cynthia, I'll never keep anything from you again."

"There are no more secrets," she says.

"There are none. I promise."

She smiles. "You don't think I didn't know you faked your death this whole time?"

"I mean, that William faked his death—that you are—that you've . . . always been." Amidst streams of salty tears, their lips find each other.

He leaves her alone in the office. When she opens the shoe box he leaves behind, she finds notebooks filled with even penmanship compiled by Theo. She also finds the notes leading up to the whereabouts of the Drake Family, including the location of the Goose's likely hideouts. There is a map with hundred of locations around the world, places where the Goose has opened up his chain of restaurants. Underneath the map, Bryant had written, "Where is the Goose hiding?"

She empties the box, and at the bottom of it all, she finds a necktie with the same green and gold plaid as the vest William Lately wore when she started falling in love with him, before his death, and before she saw him hanging from her sprinkler.

The Duke comes barreling out of his private villa, the only asset he has left after the incident with Darla. He was left responsible. And now he's shirtless, furious, and carries a crimson red baseball bat. He says, "You . . . . What . . . ? Who . . . ? Is someone there?"

Moments later in the distance he hears, "Whooo . . . ." But there's no other sound, so the Duke tells himself, "It's just a sound from the winds on the hills."

When he returns inside his home, there's a note on the table. The note is comprised of scratches that read, "I've been . . .

watching you." He panics and knocks over things from his dining room table; a candle must have fallen over and burned the carpet. He tosses his wine on the fire and puts it out. He says, "Who is it? Hello? This isn't going to work. I'm not going to open the door."

He doesn't need to open the door either, for when he looks out the window again, the Brood lands, together and all at once, on a sturdy tree with its thick trunk. The Brood covers the tree's branches that conceal the front of the Duke's house from the road. When they stretch out their wings and spread them wide, a message is revealed to security cameras on the villa property and to the Duke himself. Among the patterns on their wings, the message clearly and simply reads, "I am the Brood." To his astonishment the Duke cannot stop from racing out the door. He dashes outside and says, "Who on Earth is the Brood?"

Of course, the owls close their wings, except for those that have the letters that make up the words: "I am."

An owl flies over the stone roof of the villa complex, dropping a newspaper clipping onto the ground at the Duke's feet. The clipping tells . . . the story of the legacy of a great inventor.

The clipping reads: "—skilled developer M. Hollindais may have a solution. But with the inventor missing, the world has had to turn their sights elsewhere to find answers for the growing concerns Hollindais worked to address—"

"Hollindais?" asks Cluster.

The owls hoot loudly.

"The Brood," says Cluster, "you've turned to me of all people. I am grateful that you have selected me to fund your research. But there's one thing I can't figure out—Why should I help you with anything?"

The Brood moves from the trees to the sky in one swarm of perfectly timed swoops and flaps of their many sets of wings. The owls circle together . . . in the sky.

"Where are you going? I wasn't finished talking with you . . . . Wait!" exclaims the Duke of Framingham.

From the sky, with their sharp talons wide, the Brood drops from the large circle formation into a downward spiral of feathery flight. When they meet it is around the basket of flowers that the Duke took from the bedside of Dr. Cynthia Valentico when the Duke visited her in the hospital after Darla's passing. The birds proceed to rip the wicker basket apart without any resistance, and the wooden pieces come down like hail from a landmine.

"You know about what that witch doctor did to me, and to my-my . . . my Darla," so says the Duke. "Oh my Darla . . . ." He nods in devotion. "I'm at your side . . . if you will help me dispose of the person who wrecked my life."

In her home office, Cynthia puts on her yellow cardigan, and she takes open her desk drawer to work on a case. Stegner calls her and tells her about his suspicions surrounding the case. He tells her all about the case that Theo has been prepping. Theo bursts in the room and says, "Now you have time to talk!?"

"I came out to see you a moment ago, but you were asleep," says Cynthia.

"I was napping," says Theodore. "Listen, something is going on in the department. We've got to get to the bottom of things."

"You're telling me," says Stegner. "You stay out of this, Bryant."

"You're calling my home phone, Larry," says Theo.

"It's not my fault *our* Internal is run by a shrink who lives with a nut-job writer," says Stegner.

"Did you forget how I got my badge back when you tried to take away my right to investigate?" asks Theo.

"No," says Stegner. He calms down and tells Cynthia about the incident with the dignitary who was going to the Montréal Climate Control Summit. The dignitary never made it to the summit when she was taken prisoner and put in the back of a squad car belonging to the Force. The car was signed out and taken from the department when things were in turmoil. Lady Raindaleigh never made it to the summit to hear the scientists speak about the strange Elixiumbrium Crystals, and how they would help restart the tides. "You're god damn right. I got one dead cop and an unexplained conspiracy on my hands, while you're off changing diapers with Detective Bryant . . . ?" begs Stegner, over the phone.

"Alright, Cap," says Cynthia, dismissively. "I'll see what we come up with."

"You're going to have to end the call if you want my opinion," says Theo.

"What?" asks Stegner. "You think I had something to do with this?"

"I found it odd that you showed up to the scene just before Sergeant Bill Hutchinson panicked and knew his cover was blown," accused Theo.

"I showed up as soon as I got the call that shots were fired," said Stegner. "We were all patrolling the area."

"Oh really," says Theo. "Can you tell me what car you were patrolling in?"

"What car?" asks Stegner. "You know my car, Bryant. It's the . . . . It's . . . ."

"What number car do you have?" inquires Cynthia.

"413," says Stegner. "But I had to . . . sign out a car that day."

"You're a suspect in this, too, Larry," says Theo. "Tell him you'll get back to him."

"I'll get back to you, Larry," says Cynthia.

"No, wait—" says Larry before Cynthia hangs up the call.

The fly guts on the wall from earlier draw Theo's attention. "You're going to have to explain this," he says to her.

"I'm going to—A cop is dead. And the dignitary is free, but she doesn't know anything, and you're telling me Stegner might be in on it."

"No," says Theo. "I just didn't think he had anything to contribute."

"Okay," says Cynthia.

Theo tells her how Bill Hutchinson was working with someone: "The cop who was shot and whoever else—not Stegner, but some cop . . . who hasn't got much else to lose. They were hired . . . to interrupt the dignitaries. That's what Stegner is having trouble understanding."

"I guess he's not the only one," says Cynthia.

"It took me some time to figure out," says Theo, "but there are two sides in this. There is the committee who was meeting to fix the tides, and there's the people . . . who don't care about fixing the tides. Those people who want the world to be *destroyed*. I think they were paying Hutchinson and whoever else to intercept the foreign dignitaries and prevent the . . . ."

"But who would do such a thing?" asks Cynthia.

"I'm not sure," says Theo, "but they have been at it . . . for a long time. Luckily, there are some other people . . . who've been at it longer."

"Too bad both sides will do anything they need to do to get their way," says Cynthia.

"What do you mean?" asks Theo.

"Listen to this," says Cynthia. She plays a news report about an incident that happened at the Montréal Climate Control Summit, where an engineer was shot. "Hold on," she says. She calls Stegner on the phone. "Do you know anything about the man shot at the climate change convention?"

Stegner pauses and says, "Yeah . . . ? Let me guess . . . . You've finally figured out I'm not in on it . . . . And now you need my help . . . ?"

"We knew you were clean, Larry," says Theo. "Cripes. Take a look in the mirror, friend. You're the cleanest character of them all."

"Well," says Stegner, "I'll accept your apology."

"That wasn't—" says Theo before Cynthia whacks him on the knee. "What did you hit me for—"

"I'm wondering . . . if there was a connection. I mean obviously the two incidents are connected," says Cynthia.

"Well," says Theo, "obviously . . . . They are . . . . Because . . . . "

"Because the people who *hired* Hutchinson and whoever else must have wanted to keep the dignitaries away from the convention—Because they didn't want them to get to see the engineer who was shot—"

"Yes!" exclaims Theo. "He was shot when all the Force, every cop in Montréal, was out scouring for Lady Raindaleigh."

"The engineer . . . was," says Stegner but he's lost. "You said they hired Bill?"

"Yes," says Theo. "We'll catch you up later."

"Wait—" says Stegner, and Theo nearly hangs up the phone before Cynthia pushes him away. "You're going to have to catch me up quick because the old engineer, Oriel, he's still alive—"

"Great," says Theo. "Tell him we're on our way."

John Cluster "the Duke" Drake chose his nickname after his family name became a common commodity. The Drake Family was known for their fortune and the infamous Loose Goose Saloon was their mascot. Anyone that knows the Duke should sympathize with the resentment he must carry toward the Goose for ruining his family namesake. The Brood plays on that very resentment and fuels it by rekindling the Duke's conscious hatred toward Valentico. It's easier to turn him toward her, and the Brood hopes that the spark will be enough to light a fire for the others. He hopes to send a signal to Valentico and Theo, not to hurt them or have the Duke hurt them, but he hopes they will help Oriel figure out a way to end the Drake Family by any means necessary. So the Brood remains stationed in the trees that surround the Duke's private villa.

The Duke spends some time trying to convince himself that he had a vivid imagination. But the next day the owls are still there, and they follow him when he drives his motorcycle to town. They wait outside of the club when he goes to get a drink, and they are there when he returns to his private villa.

"I would do anything to avenge her death," said the Duke of Framingham, as he went out to talk to the Brood. "You'll have to pardon me . . . . I haven't tried talking to birds since I was a boy, but I guess not much has changed. If you were who you say you are . . . that inventor guy," He finds the clipping on newspaper on the ground from earlier. "If you're this Hollindais guy, why are you willing to help me do . . . terrible things to these people."

The Brood doesn't respond, but an individual approaches from behind the tree the Brood occupies. "My name isn't important," says the individual right away. He's dressed in black and quite assertive. "I've assisted Hollindais when he was a man. And he was captured . . . when I was on leave. So this is how I must repay the man . . . . He'd do anything to get their . . . attention."

"Wait," says the Duke. "I thought he needed some of my money to fund experiments."

"It's not always about the money," says the individual. "What the Brood needs . . . is to get Detective Theodore Bryant away from helping the Oriel Family."

"Where do I fit in?" asks the Duke. "You say the Oriel Family. I could care less about the Oriel's, since my Uncle Gino is making that his own life's purpose."

"If you have allegiance to your family, perhaps we've come to the wrong person," says the individual. He steps away and the owls take to the sky.

"I have no allegiance," says the bitter Cluster. He puts it bluntly, "If you both want the same thing as the Goose, that scum—I got you covered. We can work together on it." He shakes hands with the individual as the owls resettle on the branches above them as before. "Just so long as I get my chance to hurt Valentico. I want her to see someone she loves perish," says the Duke. The individual backs away from the Duke, as the Duke directs his energy to the sky and the tree branches, by saying, "I want her to know what my pain is like!"

"Why, if you need your revenge," says the individual, suddenly peaking from behind the tree, "you will . . . get your chance for it." The individual moved completely behind the tree.

When the Duke goes to investigate where he went, the individual is nowhere to be found. But the Brood is still all around him, in the branches above the Duke's head. "Perhaps there's a way to turn you back," says the Duke. "If you were turned this way, then there might be a way to reverse the effects."

When the Brood is reminded of the dream of returning to his old form as a human being, he takes the Duke to a remote part of the forests of Wimble. There, they stand near the fallen archway to a cemetery, next to the Duke's motorcycle that will not make it through the chained gate. The Duke stays there until he sees the Brood flying overhead, and he follows to see what the mystery is about:

Upon a marble statue rests a pine box where the Brood

lands and surveys until the Duke gets there. When the Brood moves away from the box, the Duke opens it to find that it's a small coffin for a single owl.

The Duke says, "Well, I suppose you can't reverse something that isn't quite whole to begin with."

The Duke is right about what it takes to be complete, for he, too, knows the woeful feeling of being incomplete, without the love of his fiancé. The Brood preyed upon the Duke, and his bodyguard, Tyre, purposely left out one very important detail: The real reason the Brood needs Cluster and had to get Theo & Valentico's attention by any means possible. He needs the old engineer named Oriel to believe the Brood is in fact the inventor. Most people aren't desperate enough, as the Duke is, to accept the Brood is who he says he is. It took more convincing to get Tyre's attention. The more that Oriel hears about the Brood's existence, from Tyre himself, and from other people, the more Oriel will believe, and they'll need to work together . . . if they are to mend the planet.

The Duke puts on a clever disguise and goes to make an appointment to see Dr. Cynthia Valentico. He thought he could just walk right in, but Cynthia has a receptionist keeping people from entering. She had hired the receptionist after the incident with Darla Henderson, of course. And the receptionist denies the Duke, who's Russian Cossack-style hat makes a poor impression. The receptionist is a vegan, so the Duke's clever disguise is a bust. She keeps him from entering by saying, "I'm sure the doctor can assist you, but you'll need to follow our strictest standards of new patient entry." She gives him guidelines to make a video to tell the doctor about his case.

The Duke takes that information to mean that he should create a scenario in which the doctor must respond to a new client in distress. To make the video recording seem authentic, the Duke hires an actor to pretend to be a child in distress.

"It's for a short film I've been working on as a side project with a few filmmaker friends," says the Duke. "We're filming the teaser." He ushers in the next family to audition for the part, but he's only concerned about how the child looks on camera. "The child's cry will be what will drive Cynthia to respond to the call for help," thinks the amateur filmmaker to himself.

An old film set, with low overhead costs and perfect eerie lighting, is the place they stage the shoot. The scene of an abandoned farmhouse, with liquor bottles spread over the floor and a strange chemistry set on the table, suggests drug production.

The child's voice says: "I have to be quick . . . before my parents get home from work. I'm alone and all I want is to get out of here. Please help." When the door starts creaking open—the Duke adjusts the sound by adding a prerecorded track. He captured the sounds of old tree limbs swaying in a forest— the sound appears to come from behind the child, who follows the script by screaming, and that's when the faux snuff film cuts to black.

"The trap is set. All we need to do now is wait for it to be sprung," says the Duke to a tree filled with owls.

He told the camera how he slept alone most nights out of fear that his father would think he was weak for wanting to sleep near his mother or sister. He was a young boy still, and he told the camera how he felt his father would say something stern, something like, "No matter how you hide it, you're weak." So the young monster slept alone.

He had his favorite two possessions, and he told the camera, privately, about how he would sleep alone with just his knife and wool blanket. He would sleep at their lair, or he would sleep at a gathering fire, or he would sleep near a trap if he was really tired. But he was never really asleep, he claimed. He told her about his fears.

"I was afraid the trap was under me and I would fall in on my own traps like the man my father told me about so many times. I guess I didn't want to bring shame to our family," said the monster.

Dr. Cynthia Valentico responds to the video interview she believes a child had sent to her. She tells her own camera a story to give the child hope. She tells what shame means to her: "When I was a child, my mother brought me to a field of flowers, and she told me I could pick and bring any flower to class with me later that day. Of course," says the doctor, "I picked the biggest, fullest flower. A tulip I spotted from our walk up the hill. I can remember my mother's excitement and joy over me recognizing the beauty in nature. She said, 'Don't worry if it doesn't survive. If another kid ruins it. Or if your teacher throws the flower away when you go to lunch. You picked this one, so you can pick it again. You have a knack for beauty.' Perhaps you have a knack for trapping animals, young man."

The boy appears to respond the next day. The dark video feed is of silhouette, where the doctor can see the boy is looking down. He collects her story and tries to apply it to himself. He speaks quietly, almost in an aside to himself. He says, "I picked something beautiful, too." Then, her video screen goes blank.

"It's something that happens sometimes," Valentico thinks aloud. The video transmission sometimes comes through poorly because the internet happens to be redirecting their IP address all over the planet for the sake of anonymity. Cynthia is aware that anonymity works both ways, so she doesn't doubt her strict procedures.

As of now, Dr. Valentico is more than acquainted with Detective Theodore Bryant. It seemed natural for them to pursue a romantic partnership after the fair. And they married at the same time Theo left the Force, which was during The Case of Sylvan Trappers. Cynthia feels this strange child on the video echoes the Sylvan Trappers, so, naturally, Cynthia rushes to Theo after the strange encounter with the distressed young child.

When Detective Theodore Bryant arrives at the scene, he's alone. "Where's Valentico?" asks the Duke. "You promised me the doctor, and we get this twit instead?" The Brood ruffles its feathers at once. The Brood prepares to deliver some message to Theo, but the Duke puts a stop to that when he captures one of the owls in a cage, and puts it in the basement of his private villa.

The Brood thought he would outsmart the Duke by gaining the detective's attention, but he knows if he goes through with his plan, the Duke will harm another part of the collective unit that makes up the Brood, and he already knows what it feels like to have part of him die off. The remaining owls wait in the tree tops again. They bide their time there.

"Strange how owls seem to congregate like that," thinks

Theo to himself.

The Duke speaks to the remaining owls: "We have to take one . . . of . . . take one of two strategies here. We're the house, and the house . . . always wins. Either we take something she loves from her . . . by doing away with this foolish detective . . . . Or better yet, we can take them both . . . if we somehow get Bryant to come back with his wife."

"This is history repeating itself, huh?" asks the Duke when he reads the clipping left for him of an article written by a reporter named Jackie Danzel. In the article, Danzel exposes the case of the Sylvan Trappers and what the couple went through, including how it was Theo's last case with the department, and the marriage that came from the emotional stakes placed upon Cynthia and Theo. Danzel wrote:

"That was when Detective Theodore Bryant took Cynthia by the hand, and he looked at their hands together. She noticed and smiled at him. He started doing a funny thing with his breathing that made it seem like he was trying to say something but couldn't find the words."

Theo is in Cynthia's sedan with her and thinking to himself how this time is different. He looks up from their hands at her sweet face and tender lips.

Then, he notices something strange about the park next to their home. He says, "I've never heard of that many owls . . . moving in groups. They're usually . . . solitary."

"Strange," says Cynthia. "How absolutely strange of you to come back to talk about owls."

"No," says Theo, and he smiles proudly. "I came back last time because I wanted to marry you. I think a lot about raising our child together, and I want you both to be safe. When I was looking for that boy and his family today, I felt like I was close to something. But if anything were to happen when I'm not around . . . . Something from another case even. I don't want to take those risks now that everything is perfect."

"Okay," says Cynthia. "Let's get Alan someplace safe. We'll take him to your mother's. She has a panic room if anything goes wrong."

"And you," says Theo.

"Come on," says Cynthia. "I should be there with you. Then we'll both be safer. Partner?"

"I was already protecting you," says Theo.

"Alright," says Dr. Valentico. "We're already married, so I may as well come with you . . . like the last time."

"Okay," says Theo, "sounds good to me. There's no real danger if the child's family isn't around, I suppose."

The Brood moves out fast when it sees the cavalry of police moving over the hills with their weapons raised; the owls think they've fulfilled their end of the deal without much resolution on the Duke's end, so they leave the Duke of Framingham to fend for himself.

With the Brood gone, the Duke is trapped in the place he imagined he would see his plight of vengeance carried out. He slips into his own trap he had set for Theo and Cynthia to fall into. He's bleeding profusely when all he can do is imagine what that would have been like to watch from above. He shouts above the storm brewing in his own mind, for Theo, Cynthia, and the four-dozen pairs of pursuing members of the police department to hear: "Oh my Darla! You belong to me! You belong . . . to me!"

Theo starts to say, "It's over Duke of Fram—" When Cynthia interrupts him to say: "How dare you hold Darla's death over my head—She tried to kill me, and all I ever wanted . . . was to help that poor woman." Theo holds her as the Duke gargles and gurgles and gags on a mouthful of his own blood.

"What happened to the Duke when he fell into his own spiked trap was his unfortunate fate," Cynthia tells reporters.

Both her and Theo would keep wondering what became of all the owls, especially after a strange man dressed in black came out of the Duke's home with a cage and set one owl free in front of them.

"Are you the one putting the owls everywhere?" asked Theo.

"I have fulfilled my duties," said the man. "Now you must . . . fulfill yours."

CASE SEVEN:

Captain Stegner felt it was absolutely without a doubt necessary to bring Theodore Bryant in to work on the case, even though he handed his badge back to Stegner after the case of the Sylvan Trappers had come to a close. He felt that Detective Theodore Bryant and Dr. Cynthia Valentico were the only ones that shared enough ingenuity and thorough capability to match the intensity for the case Cary Oriel brought to the captain. The same case, along with other procurements in this volume, is part of the true-crime saga called *Asleep in the Skies*.

Briefly interviewing Inspector Cary Oriel himself, in his home and at a diner outside of Ottawa, Captain Larry Stegner evaluated Inspector Cary Oriel's situation. He was cautious about the inspector, since Cary was the son of the old engineer. He spies the middle-aged inspector holding back bursts of sorrow and fear for his children and the old man, who simply went by Oriel.

The inspector had returned to Montréal not long after the incident at the Montréal Climate Control Summit, when the old engineer had been shot. Luckily, the old man was a clever pioneer of invention, who always wore an impenetrable vest while speaking publicly. He survived the attack, only to go missing a day later. The disheveled inspector from Never York escaped from the people who were looking for his family's secret discovery, known as Elixiumbrium Crystals.

Inspector Oriel happened to become acquainted with Captain Stegner in a strange way that is thoroughly detailed in *Asleep in the Skies*. When Cary Oriel turned to Stegner for help, the captain feared the bureaucracy but contemplated bringing Cary into the station to start examining his case there, until Cary mentioned a discovery of his own. Cary's discovery during his inspections linked the Loose Goose Enterprise to the gang of crooked cops and seedy lowlifes who had been the cause of Cary fleeing from Never York City in a hurry. He even rode in a cold boxcar to escape being mangled by the baddies.

Uncertain if the precinct in Montreal was a safe place for Cary, Captain Stegner decided to take control of the situation. He pulled his cruiser over at a diner, and after Cary unraveled inside, he was forced to lock the inspector in the back of the cruiser. Captain Larry Stegner raised his mug to block the glare beaming into his eyes when he proposed to Inspector Oriel that he knew the perfect team for the job.

He tried to prove his hunch to Oriel, who was immediately shocked that Stegner would suggest bringing in another person to work with after he had already seen so much corruption.

"Do you really think another person coming in and taking a look will really shed some light on this? I've had nineteen departments across the East Coast, leading up to yours, look into it. Why don't we just look over this Bryant? Ex-police sergeant . . . ? Let's look at his files together first, alright?" said the agitated Oriel. He was tired of forcing his way, but he was resilient to make a point. He said, "I need to keep as few people on this since I'm here and someone is after me."

"I understand your frustration, I do," said the captain. "But I'm not bringing in one person."

"Good," said Cary.

"I'm bringing in his wife too."

Inspector Cary Oriel gulped. He looked outside the back window of the cruiser. It was a stone building, where, in the snow, some tracks pointed to their small shed in the dark, icy woods. It was where Captain Stegner claimed they would have such a remote and guarded place of tranquility, "Far from any bastard without buckshot for blood."

Inspect Cary Oriel had a moment in the car where, in the backseat behind the bulletproof glass and wire mesh, the inspector quietly spoke aloud, as if in a trance.

"Why are you doing this to me?!" Cary shouted. Oriel looked over at the seemingly empty seat next to him. He stayed looking, rather longingly, before reaching for someone who wasn't there with him. At least not in physical form.

"Listen to me, Oriel," said Stegner, "if you saw people are after you . . . . Are these people I can see?"

"Yes," said Cary.

"Then maybe we should hurry up and get to it then. Nobody knows we're here," said Stegner. "Let me tell you why Theodore Bryant . . . and his wife are the perfect pair. Theodore Bryant wasn't a detective at the time, but he was there at the border with all the other customs officers, and he was seasoned at the job."

"He's a customs officer? But I don't have any paraphernalia. I promise," said Cary.

"Good to know you're clean, and can still cut up, inspector," said the captain. "He was in charge of his unit, as a captain there, which is why he thought he could boss me around when he came over to the department. You got me so far?"

"Yes," Cary nodded.

"Okay," said Stegner. "Well, let me start with his background back at Border Patrol, why he was ideal for the department—he was the guy that came by and took orders based off of the scene, so he would react to any discrepancy a line-officer had with travelers. I remember him telling me about why he left, and why he needed more— He needed a bigger role after one case had him on the hunt to return a young child and end a ring of smugglers."

DETECTIVE THEO & DOCTOR VALENTICO
IN
A STORY OF A MISSING CHILD AT THE BORDER

"WHAT DO YOU MEAN—HE SAW SOMEONE'S KID GET TAKEN?" asked Cary with a bottom-lip full of his only ounce of restraint.

"Worse," said Stegner. "He knew a man who watched a kidnapper leave-off with this man's daughter. I hope he can get us started in the right direction. He would oversee the line-officers. They're a mix of cadets and seasoned officers sprinkled throughout the line, to keep it running smooth as a chain all greased up."

"The people doing inspections at the borders and airports . . . ?" inquired Cary.

"It wasn't much of a detective role," admitted Stegner. "They were limited in how far their jurisdiction went, so he left that to join the Force!" He crunched snow, deep to his ankles, to get to Cary's door and unlatch it from the outside. "But the guys doing greetings— They do inspections and greetings, but most people see the customs officers as an inspection train— I'm saying half their job is customer service. Any department store clerk can do their jobs, just like any department store manager could run the place."

"It's a miracle that your department hired this guy," said Cary, who calmed down enough to have a smile. "Where is he meeting us?"

Captain Larry Stegner continued telling about Theodore as they made their way through a dusty trail that lead under snow covered trees. "Bryant enjoyed his time as a line-officer and running the border station. Probably felt like he played a part as an ambassador to Canada." He paused walking, and they watched one snow covered tree lose its well-balanced icecap. A massive, mostly solid lump of snow fell before their feet. The tree's white coat freed it up to be a girth of needles wrapped in ice and plenty of bare branches beneath its thick top half.

When the light dusting that followed the ton of falling snow cleared enough for the two men to trudge farther into the thick, dark woods, Stegner said, "It wore away at Bryant eventually. Six months after his hellish time starting with the Border Patrol—after having tourists hiss and treat him like a nuisance over and over, when they were mostly taking orders from their department leaders, rather than actively searching through belongings . . . . Cadets aren't a nuisance according to the law because they're legally not harming, injuring or disturbing any of the passersby. But the leaders might prompt a cadet to take on a nuance like that."

THEODORE BRYANT put his face behind double-paned reflective glass after he made it out of the cadet role. Officers don't last all that long at BP&C since the job is so monotonous. Most officers try to find another role in the system early on. Bryant's six month promotion wasn't all that uncommon.

"As a cadet he did his job right. He once stopped some person from entering the country who had contraband, but they were polite, so, you know," said Stegner, while making a shooing motion with his gloved hands. "I remember him telling me some of the exceptions he made when he came into the station as detective. Apparently, it was both human nature and part of their training procedures to give a hard time to travelers who are rude and impolite."

"Right," added Cary. "I bet in most fair practices throughout the world that are looking for signs and signals, it is an indication; to be rude is to be untrustworthy."

Theodore Bryant appeared from around the narrow bend that could have taken Cary Oriel and Stegner off the mountainside if they hadn't heard Bryant say, "It never occurred to me that polite ones would be more sinister, until I met the man I mistakenly believed to be a father of the girl he kidnapped." They joined Theo at the edge of the mountain's slope for a perfect view of a ski-town that had passed its prime. Some skiers down below huddled near a fire underneath the lift that was still hanging. The lift was quiet in its motions, and some skiers climbed up the hill opposite of the inspector, the captain, and the detective.

. 🟊 .

Electric lights poured over the summit, higher than the cables that were used to run the lift. The lights were shining from thirty feet or so, in addition to how high the cables were. Skiers braved the snowy surface late into the night. They left marks on the snow that would fade away before the next skiers passed over. That disappearance was soothing to watch, so they stayed there and Theodore Bryant eventually said, "Mr. Underbrough, who appeared to be a gentleman, dressed as a worker in muddy overalls but he sounded well-off. I heard Cadet Blake ask . . . what his business was coming into the country."

Blake had a short military haircut and thick-framed glasses; he was an eager sort of cadet that had enthusiasm for being a part of the process. He woke up every morning with extra time to starch and iron his uniform. He was lucky to have a young wife with a child already. The twenty-two-year-old Blake kissed them both when he went to work that morning, when his tiny child spilled a bowl or cereal. It splashed onto the floor and covered his pant legs with cold milk. No child deserves to see their father storm off to change and hear those nasty words, so he thought about making a change in his heart to slow down when those things happened that he couldn't control.

Later on, when the polite workman came to the customs counter, he said his name was Mr. Underbrough. And he lifted his child and said, "She's been sick." He didn't say much about any sort of thing, which wasn't unusual since most people were tight-lipped at the BP&C Station.

"We're going to see a specialist a little farther up," said Underbrough, and the corners of his lips turned upward as he looked under the hood of the child's jacket. He examined the little girl's bloodshot eyes.

"Did she look ill?" asked Cary. He tightened his fists and he let himself cry for the first time, since Henry and Emily had went missing. He said, "Oh my little Emily. My baby girl. What did they do?"

"It wasn't much I could see wrong where I stood, sir," said Theo. "The officer on the line did his job right. He looked for all the tells—any sign—that would seem like rash behavior on the man's face. He never . . . gave it away."

His tan work jacket with thick lining had hardly any wear to it. Cadet Blake didn't take notice of anything unusual when Underbrough rocked his daughter back and forth in his thin arms. "It's four more hours," he said to the girl, "until we can get her to safe refuge." He patted her back and looked to the cadet for a word of wisdom or parting gesture.

"That's a long ride," Blake commented. Blake smelled the rotten, stale odor of sour milk, and he assumed it was left on his clothes from earlier. He shuddered with frustration. The frustrated young cadet searched deep within himself to remember the way he reacted earlier that morning. He looked for the energy to resist the temper he had shown his child, and he longed for when he would see his own child again. He told himself to keep his child smiling and happy above all other things. Seeing the workman caring for the girl certainly went far with Blake, that day. He decided he would stop getting mad about the cereal policy he was usually enforcing at home. He scanned Underbrough's American Passport.

In the next room over, Lead Officer Bryant zoomed in on a computer screen. He oversaw the approval of appropriate watermarks along the seal on Underbrough's passport. He watched the automated searches on the monitor go through a series of diagnostic tests that checked for felonies or arrest warrants on incoming travelers, but the results didn't have anything to display for Underbrough. "Hold onto passport and ask about the child's documentation," Bryant muttered standard procedure into a microphone that was mounted above the video monitor. The private room was a glass portal, where the whole operation was made visible to Lead Officer Bryant.

"Sir," said Blake, "may I see your daughter's documents?"

Underbrough was rocking her and soothing the little girl when he said, "She left it with her mother, unfortunately." She was latched onto his shoulder with her chin, and her arms were by her sides in the puffy white coat she wore. Her face had a bluish tint along her cheeks. It was a cold January morning, but the girl had more clothing and a thicker jacket than her keeper.

The line coming in the door was long, and another fleet of busses pulled up behind the full charter bus. They waited to release their passengers into the frigid air, before entering the cozy warmth of the BP&C Station. "She needs a doctor," Blake said into his radio after turning away from Underbrough and child.

Bryant gave the order to let the pair go ahead to the next phase of the inspection process: the passive observation stage.

2

So they sat together on a log and watched the skiers finish up that night's journey. With eyes of curiosity on the people that looked so tiny from way up high, like watching falling stars. Those brightly burning, red-hot space rocks are hard to miss when you're looking at the sky already.

Observations at the Border Patrol & Customs Station was no different. If someone were hiding something, most people would show it. Some even got as red in the face as a the outer-limits of a supernova. But most people developed some idiosyncratic responses to help release their worries through nervous behaviors. When people enter the BP&C, they felt the burn of bright light focused on them, for they are under a sort of microscope. Every movement, every gesture, and any strange posture was documented, and any customs official had the right to challenge an individual entering the station. They could use evidence against individuals to delay them from traveling onward.

Thoughts like these manifest and dormant fears rush forward in people's minds. "Could I have left anything in my bag to cause suspicion or concern?" People wait as the inspections continue and continue to worry over potential contraband, unclaimed or forgotten in a parcel belonging to somebody. It's enough of a contemplation to cause the calm to quiver with nervous jitters.

The day that Henrietta came through customs in that brute's care was high on the mind of Theodore Bryant's thoughts, as he sat on a log up with Stegner and Cary Oriel. He tried to remember every event he could recall about the day in hopes that some new trigger would come to his mind.

Meanwhile, on the other side of the ski resort, in a warm cabin, near a soft mattress with a beautiful woman under the sheet and waiting, sat an individual who watched Theodore Bryant and his group. From up high, the resort seemed alive with activity. The man continued watching Theo and his group walk along the La Cabane Ski Trail and head right where he wanted.

The woman took the sheet and wrapped it around her. She went to the door and opened it. "Did you hear a knock?" she asked the man with the binoculars. "Room service came," said the man. She picked up a plate and removed the silver serving dish cover before stabbing her fork into roasted red-skin potatoes covered in olive oil. "They must have ran off when you answered," said the lovely woman. "Why?" asked the man. "You weren't scared of me when we met."

"Well," said the beauty, "I'm not the typical stranger."

"Indeed," said the man. He placed his binoculars down, and he said, "What *is* your name, dear?"

"You can call me Miss Wonderful for now," said Alice. "What are you looking at?"

"I thought I saw a shadow pass by the moon," said the man. He took another plate from the cart for himself. "You'll have to take a look."

"I don't see anything," said Alice Wonderful.

"Keep looking," he said.

A knock came on the door to their room, and Alice went to open it. To her surprise, Dr. Cynthia Valentico was there on the other side of the door. "Are you comfortable here, Alice?"

"I am," said Alice Wonderful.

"You're here for invasive therapy, Miss Wonderful," said Cynthia. "I think having men in your room is breaking our deal."

"Just this one time," said Alice. "I promise he's the last one. He's . . . so strangely attractive."

"Well," said Cynthia, "I don't think it's going to help your case if you're seeing someone already. I need you to demonstrate some restraint around men in this town if you want me to sign off on you coming out of your erotomania phase."

Flynn Flannery budged in through the door and said, "As your attorney, Miss Wonderful, I advise you to cease seeing this man immediately. If you think they're not going to take your entire estate, if you start gallivanting around . . . with this. Hey . . . buddy!" Flynn Flannery moved closer to the guy with the binoculars. "You bird watching? Or what? I'm talking to you." The guy didn't move. "I can see your badge from here." The lawyer turned toward Alice Wonderful before leaving the room, and he said, "Just because he's a cop doesn't make it any better."

"McKindley? Is that you?" inquired Cynthia once Flynn stepped out in the hall to speak to his client. "What are you doing here?"

"I'm on vacation, doctor," said McKindley. "I'd like to ask you the same question."

"I've been working with Alice," said Cynthia.

"She said her name is Miss Wonderful," said McKindley.

"Well, she's a client from down south in Miami," said Cynthia.

"Wealthy woman," said McKindley.

"Yes," said Cynthia. "She's had to travel here with me . . . for further treatment. I hope you're not with her . . . just because she owns half of the luxury condos in Miami."

"She's what?" asked McKindley. "She's lovely. That's what she is . . . . And her room . . . has a great view." He went back to watching Theo and his group, still walking along La Cabane, nearing where the trail is suddenly cut off by fallen trees blocking their path.

"I've got to meet Stegner over some case that came his way," said Cynthia.

"That right?" asked McKindley.

"Yep," said Cynthia. "I've got to leave Miss Wonderful with you and . . . go meet them at home in my office."

"Well," said McKindley, "I'll take good care of her . . . ."

"Right," said Cynthia. She noticed a pink, lace undergarment, and she said, "She's in recovery. So . . . keep that in mind."

"Will do. Stay warm out their doctor," said Lieutenant McKindley.

When they were alone again, McKindley returned to monitoring the trail. "There she is," McKindley said.

"There who is?" asked Alice.

"That's my girl," said McKindley.

"What are you always looking out at?" inquired Alice.

"Nature," said McKindley. "Beautiful nature."

"There's plenty of it in this room," said Alice. "Don't you know I'm beautiful?"

"You are," admitted McKindley, and he massaged Alice's shoulders briefly.

"Then prove it," Alice challenged him.

"I'll show you my nature," said McKindley.

"Show me," Alice cried out.

McKindley took another look out the window at nature before removing the strap from his neck and placing his binoculars aside. He growled and tussled in bed with Alice.

The elderly folks in the Border Patrol & Customs Station were on another bus, not a charter bus but a touring bus, that was set to take the couple around to see some of the sights. Theo could remember hearing the couple talking, over the monitoring system, as he stood in the glass room. They were saying they had been married there: "Montréal holds a special spot in our hearts," the old man said. And the elderly gentleman had nothing to hide, but he still got nervous. Nerves are normal. He unbuttoned and re-buttoned his Hawaiian-shirt every time his wife spoke without him, and he wringed his hands like a wet wash-cloth whenever an official spoke to them. These were his nervous gestures, flapping of palm trees, that weren't related to anything outside his circumstances of being inside a customs office.

When he recalled joyous moments with his wife, thinking back forty years earlier, he still didn't let up his nervous inflections. Only when he talked of his daughter graduating medical school was he at ease. Oh, how it puts people at ease to contemplate a bright future. Cadet Blake thought the couple had nothing to hide, and Theodore Bryant remembered them passing through to observations. Because everybody gets nervous at the border.

His wife tried to console him: "Gene, if you keep doing that with your hands, they're going to be as soft as baby's breath."

Nearby the panicking elderly folks, little Henrietta's breathing was becoming shallow. When reports came in to the BP&C Station, nobody knew where her captor was taking the girl, or what would happen to her if they got there. They only knew she was being taken away from her family. After reviewing the footage taken from her brief stay in the customs office, Theodore could tell she wasn't yet harmed at the customs office, apart from the opium injections she was given that caused her drowsy behavior, and being ripped away from your parents certainly counted as a type of torture on its own. They didn't even know who were the girl's real parents until the call came in.

The amount of traffic that comes through Montréal's BP&C Station surprises most people. To someone working at the station, the different types of people and combinations of vehicles can become a blur to the eyes. It takes mighty efforts to pull an observation that's worth any merit. Still, the best way to observe people is to incite some drama to see how people cope with anxiety.

The traffic was quite light that day that Underbrough chose to pass through Bryant's station. Out of the four units at the station, it was Bryant's unit, himself and four line-officers and one deputy inspector, that served to stamp Underbrough's passport. Afterwards, Bryant did his duty to observe his group among the other bus passengers that all roamed about with the combined certainty of a lost puppy. Bryant recalled a car with two others that came in the other direction, as well. They were quietly making their way south in a sedan; overwhelmed by the bus-loads of people, the BP&C neglected to run the car's plates.

The traffic remained light until midday. Bryant recalled 11:04 AM to be the precise time the young girl passed through on his watch. Soon after, she was reported missing. He looked over those tapes for any hint of where they might have been going next. He reviewed the tapes so many times that when he revisited the events with Stegner and Cary Oriel, the time 11:04 AM came to his mind without much effort at all.

At 11:04 AM, a vile man passed to the observation area with a young girl that didn't belong with him. After each traveler was interviewed, he or she was permitted to roam about the waiting urea. The door of the waiting area was left open on purpose as usual, and as usual the travelers took out the door on their own, following their driver's footsteps.

When the group was outside on the other side of the

station, near the bus, BP&C Officer Bryant walked out with his chest puffed like a rooster walks through his den. His feet smacked the planked sidewalk. The walkway was clearly lined to guide people who were on their merry way. Bryant barked at the entire group: "You're going to get hit. We never said you guys could go."

Nobody in the group looked any way that didn't indicate complete complacency and a yielding to authority, not at first at least. But when Theodore Bryant looked back at the group he saw a young man who carried a stench of guilt in his expressions. The young man turned to look at the door that lead back inside the customs station, where people from the buses were funneling back inside. The young man stood still defiantly. Theodore gave his usual wave to signal for the group to enter, but still the young man did not move.

"He had longish-hair and must have been around 20-or-so," recalled Theodore. "The boy's rage and his inciting comments were a clear indication of guilt. I knew immediately . . . he was hiding something."

They searched his belongings and found what appeared to be stolen merchandise in his violin case. The 20-year-old was a perfect distraction; Bryant didn't realize the tactic at the time, or else he might have been more cautious of the other people in the bus groups that did not react like the young man.

The boy would eventually receive additional charges for "appearing to be an accessory in a conspiracy to kidnap a minor," but it was hard to pin the charge to the kid. He was set to be released on bail before anything went to court, but he was attacked in prison and cut good. In turn, he lost a lot of blood and didn't have to pay bail because he was in the infirmary. He wouldn't live to see the outside of the barbed fences.

"The group that orchestrated the kidnapping was behind the 20-year-old's murder, of course," said Bryant, "but when I tried to prove it, I was taken off the case by special orders from above. I was told that 'someone up high' was part of a chain of someone's that was keeping tabs on my investigations. I left that case officially after the kid died in prison. I hadn't thought of coming back to it, but I guess I never let it go from my mind."

"Whoever was conducting investigations," chimed Stegner, "had to have more clearance than you did. You wished the Border Patrol luck and tried to move on as a detective."

"And department leader of Internal Investigations," said Theo.

"Don't remind me," said Stegner.

"Still," said Bryant, "I wish I would have pursued the case more then." Bryant notices Cary with his head hanging low. He says to Cary, "Keep after them . . . . Your kids. They're out there somewhere."

"Well," said Cary, "if you couldn't find the girl at the border, how the heck am I supposed to believe you'll be any help finding my children?"

"Underbrough wouldn't have stood a chance if I knew it then," said Theo, "when he came through my station... But I knew my car was faster than he could run with a child. I didn't have a clue as to where find him when he was gone—No idea where to . . . start looking."

Along the La Cabane Trail, the closure forced the group to take a chance on cutting through a cavern. Once inside, however, an avalanche of snow sealed the men inside the cavern. The avalanche was startling in itself, even to Theo and Stegner who had been through similar circumstances. Cold rushes of air and darkness were enough trouble on their own. They weren't afraid of much though, since it appeared to be close enough and a common route for experienced explorers to take expeditions around the resort.

"They'll find us if we can't get out," said Stegner.

"Will they?" asked Cary. "This isn't the most obvious place to search. Is it?"

"They won't need to search," said Theo. "When the sun comes out it'll be over. We'll get out."

Before any resemblance of reassurance could settle in for Cary Oriel, the avalanche must have proved disturbing to another creature in the cave. The disturbance brought about the great roar of an animal within the cavern. The sounds brought chills to Cary.

They moved to the deepest recesses they could find in hopes of having another way out. They were exhausted, especially Cary who huffed and coughed and shivered. Hanging along the ceiling of the cavern were lights, but nearly all were out, except approximately every 10th light in roughly 100 foot sections. That prompted Theo to say, "This must be one of the old mining tunnels used back before this place was a resort."

"But lately," said Stegner, "I think it's been providing a route for skiers." He kicked at a track on the ground left from a recent pass of a pair of perfectly parallel skis.

"I beg to differ," said Theo. "Dear Captain, the tracks appear to be running like a ski does run on top of the snow, but I doubt anyone with poles in their palms could have kept their skis straight like these."

"Are you a professional alpiner now, detective?" asked Stegner.

"No," said Theo, "I'm afraid not. But if you look closely in the track you will see something not common to skis." The tracks had a specific indentation that went deeper than the impression of the ski itself. "Look here," said Theo as he picked up a small triangular object made of a hard metal. "What we have here is a 'Snow Eater Fin' typically found on the ski of a machine."

"A snow mobile," said the shivering Cary.

"Yes," said Theo, "I do believe so."

"Well," said Stegner, "I'm still not convinced." And he kicked the track once more.

They eventually came to the end of the cavern where a thick icy wall blocked their path. Escape from the other side seemed impossible.

They pounded their fists on the vertical wall of ice until Theo said, "There's no reason to . . . waste all our energy. It'll melt in the sun better than it does in the dead of night, and that's our chance to break free, perhaps. In the meantime . . . ." He crumpled up a bill from his wallet and said, "Anybody got a match? Tonight's stay is on me."

Later as they warmed by a fire, Stegner found ways to entertain, and bring the conversation around to why he enlisted Theo to help with Cary's case. He began from what he could remember of Theo parting from the Force: "In one of the ways it does pull to the senses, the putrid smell of the first person Detective Theodore found rotting for weeks, dead and trapped, was something the detective was never able to erase from his being, and it was what opened his senses to an unfriendly *evil* creature, an evil being that hunts human kind."

"This reminiscing is giving me the chills," shivered Cary.

"He went on hunting those creatures with his wife," said Stegner, "until they were destroyed entirely—even the monsters that realized their errors, the sick way they caught . . . and tortured. It was too much to bear. It was too much for one man. The detective couldn't stomach it. First he lost his badge. Then, he found the tracks . . . were not as clear as he had hoped."

"Let me see that video again," Theo had said to Cynthia before he asked her to marry him. "Really?" she sounded surprised.

He showed her where he saw a license plate in the reflection of the refrigerator as the boy on the screen opened the silver door to get something from inside that made Theo sick to think about. But there it was. The tag was of a different state than the boy had claimed to live. Often times, looking into tedious activities yields tremendous results, for when Dr. Cynthia Valentico was with Sergeant Theodore Bryant—a powerful romance was nearly crippled before it was given room to fly the way love is meant to soar when left to freely be— They were unstoppable together.

"She guided him for the last time that day," said Stegner. "Her crude, unkind sides were few, and they showed to few as well. She remained collected until they found the next clue they wanted to find. They were on a search for a vehicle pictured in the video they thought would lead them . . . to closely investigate the strange case Dr. Valentico brought to Theo while he was still in my department. The Case of the Sylvan Trappers . . . ."

Theo found the plate they saw on the video on the cover of

an old used car magazine, but that picture was pixilated and blurry.

"I surely can't see the VIN number," Theo said. "It could be another car. They could have punched the number in wrong on the site. This is no use."

"Okay," Cynthia said. "You're old fashioned, Theo. Why don't you go look in a book?"

"You're brilliant," Theo said, kissing her forehead gently.

"Don't let me down," she said to him. She kept clicking the computer mouse. "I'm not finding anything!" She was frustrated and clicking wildly. She printed the picture they had already looked at anyway.

Dr. Valentico looked through a magnifying glass. The VIN number was a blur of pixels, mostly grey and black squares. The focus was on the price of the vehicle, bold numbers read, "$2,450!" and the cover of *Classy Cars Magazine* was subtitled with, "Good Deals . . . for the right collector!"

"I've never thought of myself as an enthusiast, but I went to my share of shows when I was younger." Detective Theodore Bryant adjusted his weight between his brown leather shoes, pacing and flopping next to Dr. Valentico. She examined the advertisement under the bright light produced by the backend of Theo's pen.

"You'll hurt your eyes looking at it in black and white," said Theo. "Take a look. Full color of this week's *Muscle-Car Mag*. You told me to read something."

"You think you found out who bought it," said Cynthia. "Wait, this issue is from March. It's before the ad, Theodore, my love."

Stegner stood in front of the fire, his legs trembled to get warm, but his back stayed strong as he said, "That was the way they were before he went mad. Before the dark thoughts took over, and before he went mad and, at night, sometimes he woke thinking he was still there with that stinking, rotting, picked over flesh and bones that used to be a sweet innocent person—for all we know or anyone else knows. There's no reason to judge the dead, anyhow, not the ones that were victims, at least. Especially if the implications around their being in the wrong place . . . were merely coincidence.

"They were together in love," said Stegner, "before she found a lead on something gruesome that they needed to look into. She was still consulting for us at the station, and he was still with us too."

They knew the fire would keep them warm, and they hoped it would keep the roaring beast that lurked in the cavern far away from them. Their stories kept them calm and hopeful for their own survival. They kept their spirits high enough to stay awake.

Theo took his files and went to leave the lab after they pieced together an idea of where to go next. He assumed she would follow him all the way into harmful places, but she didn't get up.

"There's something I need to tell you," she said, behind a grey laptop screen. She lowered the screen on its hinge.

"Can it wait until we're on the road?" he asked.

"I wish . . . . I have something to keep your mind occupied on the long drive alone," she told him.

"Alone," he repeated.

"I can't go. I'm pregnant. I mean, I think I am. I'm fairly sure," she said, and she watched his face carefully.

"Well, I would have only let you come so close to danger anyway," Theo said to her. He continued, "Well, I should take you home on the way to . . . you know." He held up the print out of the license plate.

"I'm keeping it. And you can do whatever you want about it. Just know I'm okay, and you don't have to worry, Theo," she said.

"I'm afraid," Theo said, wiping the tears from her eyes with his fingers bent. "But I love you, so it's the best news. Don't cry, Doc."

He took that advertisement to the copy room, hung his coat on the hook by the door and waited a moment before copying the ad. She wouldn't tell him what the tears were for, so he got worried. He thought about the baby being someone else's for less time than it took for him to roll the magazine up. She would never

do that to him— She was quite reserved in romantic ways, even with the detective.
He wondered what made her cry as he made a copy. The green glow of the copy process was the only light on in the room when Dr. Valentico came in, still weeping.
Sergeant Theodore Bryant sensed where the conversation was going. He sensed the answer before the words came from his mouth, but, still he needed to know that instant.
"Is it—Is the . . . ? How far along do you think?" he finally asked.
"I didn't know what you'd say. I started bleeding a lot. Then, I had this feeling . . . . Two months. I've known for two months. I couldn't figure out how to tell you or how you would react. We're always so engaged in this, in our work," Dr. Valentico said.
"I love you too," are the last words he heard her say before she stayed behind. He drove away in an empty car, empty of her. He had no choice but to put everything he had into a sense of purpose to get back to her.

"Since her job at the station entailed listening to detectives that needed someone to hear them, she must have assumed that she could get away with remaining quiet about why Detective Bryant was always in her workspace," said Stegner as Cary stoked the fire in the cave with leaves. "I remember seeing plenty of people walking by her small office that she shared with human resources. I didn't see her speak to many of them . . . . I usually keep close tabs on every person under my supervision in the department, so I went to see if she was alright in her new position one afternoon. I had no idea Dr. Valentico was working *that* closely with Theodore Bryant."

It was true what he said. Captain Stegner was always watching everyone closely to make sure changes didn't need to be made. Early on when she first came to the department as a consultant to help Internal Investigations, Stegner had once asked Cynthia, "Ms. Valentico, how do you take your coffee?"

She said, "Make it like you would make a red-eye espresso drink, with a great deal of hot water. Thank you, dear."

"Sure," said Stegner, "I bet you're excited to be aboard here, doctor."

"Yes," she said, "thank you."

"We'll have half our department in your office by noon I bet," Stegner jostled her.

"No, Captain," said Cynthia. "Perhaps you should take time to read over . . . our agreement."

He read over her contract in the midst of fetching her red-eye espresso. Upon returning he said, "Might as well be hot water here. It looks like I drowned . . . some ants in a cup."

*"but did you see detective?" I expected the full report, but ~
rosin* *until at I would down in my ah ir to have to th~ that I
didn't ~'en ~ i~ vine with nt ate raneer*

"What placed the victim in your search?" the captain asked Theo when the detective returned from his first attempt at locating the Sylvan Trappers.

"I wanted to find a boy . . . . A boy . . . was in trouble," he answered the captain. His words came out listlessly.

"And how did you know this, detective?" asked Stegner. He wanted Theo to tell him on the record in front of the camera he had setup, even though he already knew it for himself. "Tell me what you told me about the doctor, your fiancé."

"We're married now, Captain. Part of my time away from that mess I walked into has been spent making good on a promise I made to Cynthia. It . . . helped to get our minds off what I saw before I told her what happened."

"What did you see detective?" asked Stegner, expecting to hear the full report, but he was growing impatient. He rooted down in his chair to show Theo that he didn't plan on leaving without his answer.

"I saw this flash of light. And there she was: my whole world. It was where we first met," he said, and he squinted at the captain. He continued, "Do you remember the case?"

"I do," Stegner told Theo. "And I remember when she nearly caused you to lose your cover at the fair."

"You put me on without considering my background," said Theo.

"Well," said Stegner, "I wouldn't do that. It seemed like you were the right fit for the job. You were used to keeping cool during border patrol inspections."

"But this was different," Theo said. He sounded belabored. He said, "Border patrol, working those inspections, people knew I was in charge, but when I was undercover . . . . You saw how Cynthia looked at me when we were undercover working the fair, Captain." He was stunned by his image of her. "She was so pure. There was no reason for you to put me on that case. It was a fortunate affair, indeed."

"Yes," Captain Stegner answered. Stegner could remember how she looked at Theo like he actually worked at the fair, even though he had been at the station and had already met her for a psych-evaluation before then. It wasn't that he was good undercover, either. "Well, you fit in at the fair, Theo," Stegner told him.

The smoke from the fire was becoming thick and fresh air was a must. Cary dampened out the fire except for enough embers to keep the space warm, while Theodore and Stegner worked on finding ventilation. Theodore took a stick that had been smoldering in the fire over near the wall of ice to try melting his way out. The torch he held melted enough of a hole to accomplish not choking on smoke any longer, but what water dripped down extinguished the burning thicket Theo held.

"Just like stubborn Bryant to try to work with a wet flame," said Stegner. He kicked at the edge of the frozen wall. It was most translucent near the wall of the cavern that faced towards the resort. "It's like the Sylvan Trappers. When I had to pressure you for a response. It was one thing to have this reaction, but the unwillingness to talk to his superior was altogether harder to tolerate."

"You lost your patience then," said Theo. The flames made his shadow appear long on the frozen wall of ice that blocked their paths. "I won't sleep with your big campfire stories." He took another stick that was on fire to the icy wall, but it burned out without the fire to support its temperature.

"That wood is wet," said Cary.

"I tried to reason with you," said Stegner. "You wouldn't tell me what you saw out there and came back to the department like nothing happened. So I put a unit on you."

"They tailed me all around Québec City," said Theo.

"I know," said Stegner, "and don't think for a moment I didn't know about your courthouse wedding."

"I got your gift in the mail," said Theo.

"How was the honeymoon?" jabbed Stegner. "Did my guys have to follow you two all the way to Niagara Falls for it?"

"Nope," said Theo. "We lost the tail and headed up north. But the Falls sounds better." Theodore showed a rare side of himself in that cave. Perhaps it's what the brashness of being trapped does to a man. He opened up to them in the cold, dark natural elements. Perhaps the detective feared the creature lurking. The elements got to Stegner, too. In the same way he felt trapped behind his badge when he tried to keep Theo from going after the Trappers.

"I don't think there was much of a trail," said Theo. "It wasn't blatant enough for your guys. They weren't ready for it. I wasn't either when I was on the Force, certainly not. Gerald and McKindley, and the rest . . . . They weren't able to manage seeing what I *forgot* to report to you."

"Alright," Stegner finally said. "We'll manage."

"I only came back to Montréal that day to give Cynthia her wedding bells because I didn't know if I had anything left to give," said Theo, as he turned away from the fire. The moon glowed outside of their cave, and its beams lit the icy wall. The glow illuminated like a lightning bug behind the glass of a jar does, just a little something to add to the visible light in a room.

"Coward," said Stegner. "I've tried to justify bringing you in, Bryant, but we're only talking with you because you and *her* are a package deal."

"I turned the MPD's Internal Investigations into what it is today," said Theo.

"It was a circus with you involved," said Stegner.

"I came to your office that day because I thought . . . you would help us," said Theo. "But you wouldn't."

When Theo was a sergeant standing in Stegner's office with his arms crossed and his hands in his pockets when his arms would relax, it was clear to the captain that Sgt. Bryant was hiding something. Stegner could tell he was doing everything in his power to keep a barrier between the cloud of graphic images he recalled, to keep them out of focus long enough to concentrate. He scratched and moved his fingers in circles behind his ears, and he moaned to himself. In his last moments as a sergeant with the Force, Theo finally reconciled, "There's no time to get into details with you. There would be no point."

Stegner pushed him by saying, "There's time for you to get married, but not enough to tell me what you're getting into?"

"Okay," said Theo, "you're right. We should talk. You're right, Captain. I just feel like rushing off by myself. It's my natural instinct to protect those I care about, I suppose. And I don't want you to see . . . I feel like ending their way of life." After much deliberation, Theo finally pronounced, "Because, there's no easy way to put it, they're going to kill more people with their traps." The Trappers were convincing Theodore to pursue the case as a rogue.

This was the very first time Captain Larry Stegner had heard anything regarding traps, trappers, or the like.

Sergeant Theodore Bryant told his superior everything he could manage to tell him that day . . . . He told him about the way the Sylvan Trappers did it, he told him of what he believed to be their motives, and he told him what he found at the scene before he couldn't handle it and had to leave.

"You heard all that, and still . . . . You couldn't help him with the case?" inquired Cary. The fire was mostly out, and the moonlight was all they had to rely upon.

"Well," said Stegner, "I told him how he needed to build an appetite before going out and seeing that kind of carnage, and he told me about the trappers . . . and their . . . insatiable appetites. This was before that reporter came in and got Theo & Valentico back out there, and we found out the truth about those strange monsters."

"And you sent them back to where they came from?"

asked Cary.

Theo was silent.

"That was you?" asked Cary.

"Yep," said Theo. He continued, guiltily, "We thought they were evil beings that hunted to kill people with their spiked poison pits, and I saw the traps they built."

"But they weren't real," said Stegner. "Those monsters weren't killing people any longer. The cruel monsters were no longer in charge. A more civilized monster was running everything. The traps they built were just for show, and to manipulate their social order. But I listened to you, and I learned how you found out about the Sylvan Trappers. I didn't approve of Cynthia being involved at that point—"

"I told you, Cynthia always came first," said Theo. "I had to bring her. She's my partner. She's a better partner than anyone I know."

"Well, I suppose it's right to drag her along," said Stegner. "She's the one who found the monsters after all. I keep forgetting. They're the doctor's work after all . . . ."

Before leaving after them and finding their traps, when he was going out of his jurisdiction as a sergeant, Theodore Bryant left and everyone who knew him anxiously awaited his return.

Despite having strong feelings of love and admiration for Dr. Valentico, Theo parted ways with her when she first saw through his meandering nature and puzzling demeanor. His provocative disposition caused emotions to run high. With a child on the way, his choice to leave to continue working on finding the Sylvan Trappers placed their relationship at a striking point.

Given Dr. Valentico's history with the close call she had with her own practice, when a patient attacked her violently, she had a vulnerable nature that was eager to love him through the haze he adopted. She was so equipped to love a man with post-traumatic stress disorder more than most women could. It's possible she was predisposed for it. When most women would have already given up and decided the man was unlovable, it was her true nature to love him.

The strange flicker inside him was something adopted by

many men and women who were in such lines of duty. At other times he was as easy to reach as an apple on a sapling planted outside the fence, when the horses have broken loose the night before. Indeed, Theo was unordinary. Unusual even. A rather polite fellow that never spat, nor called anyone anything out of line. He knew how to read a situation.

"I remember when you disappeared," said Stegner. He took a flask from his jacket pocket and had himself a quick drink. "I did entertain the notion that Theodore Bryant was on the drink," he said to Cary. He offered the flask, and Cary accepted. Stegner continued, "Or I thought he could have taken off to move to a new town. With so many people on the Force it happens those ways. When someone sees too much and goes insane, or can't handle the pressure. I prefer them to move on that way than . . . get overwhelmed and . . . ." Cary passed the flask to Theo, and Theo capped it without taking a drink. He tossed it to Stegner who finished what he needed to say with, "Ka-*blam*!"

Stegner and the rest of the department knew Theo was seeing more of Dr. Valentico than anyone else on the Force. Things started to spark up between the doctor and detective after Cynthia nearly ruined Theo's cover at the fair, when she laughed at his undercover magic act. When it came to hunting the Trappers and recovering from the images he saw, especially those his mind manifested, people weren't sure how it was possible for Theo to lose his mind with such a graceful, benevolently pure angel like Cynthia on his side. As the Karmic Wheel of Theo's life did spin, Cynthia was relentless to make sure his needle didn't spin wildly in either direction.

In Theo's last few moments as a sergeant on the Force, Stegner had questioned him based off of the assumption that the detective was out of his mind when he showed up with his story, and Stegner kept having trouble believing how he got into the mess. When Sgt. Theodore Bryant sat in Stegner's office, he took to the wood desk with his nails hitting on it, and without letting that energy fall, he picked up and paced himself around the tiny office. It was like he couldn't decide on something. "It became apparent to me," said Stegner to Theo in the cavern, "that you were deciding what to tell me about the incident, or whether to tell me at all."

They weren't that way in age, but when Theo spoke to Stegner in his office about the Sylvan Trappers, it was like a father would speak to his son. He said, "You know I got a reason to be in here, or else I'd get back in the car and drive myself, but I need your help in this, Larry. You have to give me your word that you won't try to take me off the case."

Theo didn't work homicide, not that he wasn't trained for it, but some sergeants have a natural disposition, and Stegner thought Theo didn't have the stomach for it. Stegner never tried to put him on a murder case. That's a choice that the captain had to make because some things a homicide detective sees can't be left at work. Some things follow them around.

"What bothered me," said Stegner to Theo in the icy cave, "is that you weren't allowed to even step foot, as a keeper of the law, in the district you were investigating. They had their own . . . police there."

"I was trying to make the world a better place," said Theo. "I've been on my game since then and vigilant in my pursuit, Captain. I saw that girl get taken away from her home, and when Underbrough passed through my station I vowed to never let that happen in my town, and then I went a few steps over and out of my town—out of our town, Larry—and things seemed to be much worse outside of our city."

"That was your problem, Theo," said Stegner. "It sounds like you found a lead on something that was bigger than you were. And you went out of bounds. You came to me. You thought you could get help on it from me, did ya'? You were out of your mind when it came to the Sylvan Trappers. I don't know about Underbrough though . . . . I can't speak to it. I wasn't there for that."

"I was there," said Theo. "Authorities weren't alerted until Blake's wife untied the gag around her mouth and was able to crawl to the phone. She dialed with her toes."

"Help . . . !"
"9-1-1. What is your emergency?"

"I need help.... My daughter is missing.... Help me."

Blake received the call as Theo found out that his district had to shift protocol to a strict search of all belongings larger than handbag size, looking through anywhere a child could be hidden.

He reviewed the tapes as Blake entered the office. Blake was shaken up, and it didn't help when he saw his Henrietta on the video monitor.

They took off together on a pursuit without limits of the law. Theo kept saying, "Hold on tight." He didn't know what else to say to Blake. He knew that false promises to return his daughter would be a torture of their own kind. He could only try and press that accelerator farther down, but it was down as far as it would go.

They stopped in a bar to figure out their next move. Theo was getting anxious too, so he said, "I have to tell them . . . where we went. I can't just keep saying 'I'm on pursuit' all day, can I?"

Blake looked a million miles away when he drank a shot of whiskey and another shot of gin, and he had more while keeping that bottle. Blake's idea was this: "Let's get whoever that . . . piece of garbage is . . . . I've heard of these types of people smuggling children. They're worthless scoundrels and thugs. The lowest of the low. We need to blow their operation apart. Find out where they're going. After we get my baby back." The general idea was noble, but the approach was all wrong. He threw up and passed out.

Theo said, "Pull yourself together." He opened up a file with a picture of the security footage showing Underbrough holding the child right in front of her father's station. "See that he gets home safe, alright?" he asked the bartender, who nodded. Theo placed a roll of bills on the bar for that service. He thought to himself, "If following protocol means one less person looking for that girl, then that's one less person who just might figure out where they're taking her."

"Over the counters and hoods . . . .

Into cruisers and into a downward spiral. Will what goes down ever come up? Only if you think like the enemy," Theo thought, so he did just that:

When Underbrough's car was spotted going east towards the ocean, Theodore and every other person that cared were scouring for a lead along the coast. On the way to the coast Theo made a stop before the highway became divided to look at a map to tell which direction would be the most likely route for Underbrough.

But a transmission came in: "Theo, this is BP&C Lieutenant Rick Rogers. I can't believe you're skipping protocol like this—" Theo shut off his radio.

"Alright," he said to himself, and he drove to where the shipping routes were most plentiful.

Meanwhile, in a refinery off the coast, the young girl woke up and started making a lot of noise, so the sneering Underbrough put a single pill in her mouth. He slipped the white capsule under her lip, and she quieted down promptly, but a dock worker saw the act. The dock worker became suspicious, and while towering over their car, he asked, "Are you alright little, girl?"

Underbrough had no hesitation. He unfolded himself from the car, and he stabbed the worker in the neck with the pointy tip of his umbrella. He carried that girl onto the carrier ship ahead of them as the worker kicked around a final few breaths near the edge of the dock.

Theo was nearly to New Brunswick when the report come in: "Nous avons une situation à Milford. La sécurité a trouvé un homme . . . poignardé à mort. I repeat, a man has been stabbed to death . . . ."

Theodore rushed to find the port at Milford, but he was too late to catch Underbrough and Henrietta before they boarded. He was pulling up as the large carrier ship pulled out to sea.

"When did the last ship leave port?" Theo asked a group of seadogs hunched around picnic benches and lunch pails. A dock worker jumped up from his seat and said, "I saw him. He killed Schmidt—"

"Did he have a little girl with him?" asked Theo. The worker nodded. Theo asked, "Can we catch up to them?" The worker nodded again, and he said, "I can but not with my tugboat."

"Not a problem," said Theo. They got into a speedboat. Theo took apart the boat's ignition to get it started. "You say you're legit," said the worker, and he stared at the BP&C emblem on Theo's jacket. "We're legit," said Theo. "This guy can't get away. He killed your friend and he kidnapped a child. I won't allow it to happen."

"Me either," said the worker, just as Theo twisted two sets of wires together and pressed the start button for the ignition.

They sped through the water and Theo said, "Turn your running lights off and get close." The lights turned off with the flip of a switch, except for an emergency light that Theo ripped apart with his bare hands to avoid detection. Even without the lights the worker knew the shore enough to dodge a few buoys.

The worker kept the speedboat out of the carrier's current and only dipped close to the large, flat ship once to let Theodore Bryant take hold of a rope coming off the magnificent bow above their heads. The carrier towered over their boat and frightened the worker greatly, but he kept it steady until Theo was missing from the speedboat. When the worker looked back to the carrier, the rope was taught to the ocean but Theo was nowhere to be found.

From the deep, dark waters emerged Theo. He climbed all the way up, to the carrier's deck. He quickly found out information from the labels on cargo containers. The ship was bound for several countries across the Atlantic Ocean. He signaled for the worker on the speedboat to go off, and the driver veered the vessel away without getting close enough to be spotted by the ship's captain.

The small civilian quarters on the carrier were rented out to people who didn't mind the weeks of ocean excursion that it takes to cross the Atlantic. Renting out rooms on shipping vessels is a way for people to see the ocean, and a way for the shipping company to make extra money housing travelers.

Underbrough held Henrietta close to his chest as the ship's steward greeted him and checked his ticket. Once the steward went on to talk to the next cabin down the hall, Theo emerged once more. This time he appeared behind Underbrough and stabbed him in the back, causing the wicked man to release the young girl. She fell to the hard, metal floor in a limp state.

Underbrough elbowed Theo square in the face, and blood gushed forth from his nose, but Theo was able to get a wide left hook around him, and that knocked Underbrough out flat on the ground.

Theo recovered Henrietta in his arms and searched the unconscious kidnapper.

"Hush," Theo said to the steward. "I need to see where she was going to be taken."

"I'm calling the ship's police," said the frightened steward.

"Good," said Theo. When the ship's police chief showed up he took the information Theo found regarding the precise location for where Underbrough planned to drop off little Henrietta. That information would help bring down one of the largest smuggling operations of human traffic that moved across the Atlantic Ocean.

Blake was still asleep at the bar when Missis Blake came to the door with red eyes, but she brightened up when she saw Theo holding her daughter. She said, "My girl. My baby. My Henrietta . . . . You're alive. My Henri! My baby, I love you. Mommy loves you forever."

"Tell Officer Blake I've arranged for his return, when he's ready," said Theo.

"I will," said Mrs. Blake. "But should I tell him you'll be

there to welcome him back?"

"No," said Theo. "I have to . . . move on."

"Well," said Cary, "I suppose, now, I know . . . for certain. I'm in the presence of a sleuth who will go out of his jurisdiction for the sake of justice."

"I suppose," said Stegner.

"I never work alone," said Theo. "And Stegner isn't much of a storyteller. In case he forgot to tell you, we'll need my wife to help piece your case together."

"He mentioned that," said Cary. "I wish she was here now to help us get out of this icebox."

"She's usually there when you need her to be," said Stegner.

The blind bear never had a chance. While most bears are agile even when in hibernation, all bears fear fire, except for the kind that can't see it. The scorch of embers from the branch Theo held made the creature run the other way. It more than doubled back and went clawing in Stegner's direction. Stegner moved, and he dove away from the fierce animal in time.

The poor bear hit the tip of its nose upon a rock, and it's skull slammed upon the wall of ice that Stegner had been agitating by himself. The old blind bear did a decent job of knocking loose the solid mass of ice. The once stiff icy covering had shifted nicely along the floor of the cavern, before the bear fled into the darkness.

At last the captain made a way for his foot between the icy wall and the track left by the snow mobile. The wall crumbled along the track on the ground left by the snow mobile's ski. It became easy to push along the slick, outer, melted track.

BIOGRAPHY

for Writer/Creator of

The Procurements of Sonny Valentine: All Kinds of Stories

&

Asleep in the Skies

. . . .

SHAUN VAIN lives in America but travels and writes fiction throughout the world.

He loves animals and cycling, and he's a naturalist.

Lightning Source UK Ltd.
Milton Keynes UK
UKHW042113171221
395800UK00002B/271